THE SASQUATCH MYSTERY

Trixie
Belden

Your TRIXIE BELDEN Library

1 The Secret of the Mansion
2 The Red Trailer Mystery
3 The Gatehouse Mystery
4 The Mysterious Visitor
5 The Mystery Off Glen Road
6 Mystery in Arizona
7 The Mysterious Code
8 The Black Jacket Mystery
9 The Happy Valley Mystery
10 The Marshland Mystery
11 The Mystery at Bob-White Cave
12 The Mystery of the Blinking Eye
13 The Mystery on Cobbett's Island
14 The Mystery of the Emeralds
15 Mystery on the Mississippi
16 The Mystery of the Missing Heiress
17 The Mystery of the Uninvited Guest
18 The Mystery of the Phantom Grasshopper
19 The Secret of the Unseen Treasure
20 The Mystery Off Old Telegraph Road
21 The Mystery of the Castaway Children
22 Mystery at Mead's Mountain
23 The Mystery of the Queen's Necklace
24 Mystery at Saratoga
25 The Sasquatch Mystery
26 The Mystery of the Headless Horseman
27 The Mystery of the Ghostly Galleon
28 The Hudson River Mystery
29 The Mystery of the Velvet Gown *(new)*
30 The Mystery of the Midnight Marauder *(new)*
31 Mystery at Maypenny's *(new)*

Trixie Belden and the SASQUATCH MYSTERY

BY KATHRYN KENNY

Cover by Jack Wacker

GOLDEN PRESS
Western Publishing Company, Inc.
Racine, Wisconsin

0-307-21596-2

CONTENTS

THE SASQUATCH MYSTERY

Camp on Champion Creek • 1

MART BELDEN TOSSED a log onto the campfire. Sparks exploded upward, flashing into brief, bright life against a starry sky.

Hypnotized by the miniature fireworks her brother had set off, Trixie Belden murmured a regretful "ah-h" as the sparks descended into the ashes.

The sound was echoed by her best friends, Honey Wheeler, Jim Frayne, and Diana Lynch; by her teen-age brothers, Brian and Mart; by her cousins, Knut, Cap, and Hallie Belden; and even by their chaperon, Miss Trask.

"Good job, Mart," said Miss Trask. "Not that

I'm an expert on bonfires, by any means."

"It doesn't take an expert," Mart said, "to see that this is no ordinary smoke-in-your-eyes, ashes-in-your-food bonfire. It's a fire with vitality . . . character. It's—"

"It's an Idaho bonfire!" said Honey with a toss of her honey-blond hair.

"What's the difference?" Hallie drawled. "I seem to remember plenty of good picnic fires in New York." While her parents had gone to a mining conference in Switzerland, Hallie had spent part of one summer with Trixie and her family at Crabapple Farm. Now Hallie's parents were in South America, leaving their three teen-agers to welcome their New York friends to their favorite camping area.

"My cousin has a point," said Mart. "Even on Champion Creek in northern Idaho, fire is fire. As usual, you have your heat and visible light emanating from a body during the process of its combustion. Also as usual. . . ."

While Mart trailed off into one of his more pompous explanations, Trixie thought to herself, *No, Mart, it's not usual—not at all.*

Just beyond the reach of firelight, she could hear the stirrings and rustlings of the forest and its unfamiliar inhabitants. Day hunters settled into nests and burrows. Night predators prowled.

She shivered a little and edged closer to Knut. Over six feet tall, Knut looked enough like Brian to be a brother instead of a cousin. Trixie felt comfortable with Knut, even though she hadn't seen him for years—not until this very morning.

Knut was from the handsome, dark side of the family that included her own father, Knut's father, Brian, and Hallie. His slightly waved black hair was brushed back like bird wings at rest. Firelight glinted on his unexpectedly heavy glasses. Trixie had assumed that Knut would have something close to X-ray vision. After all, during Hallie's visit, she had spoken Knut's name with unabashed pride each time she mentioned him. On the other hand, Hallie called Cap "birdbrain," and that didn't fit, either.

Trixie pictured a meeting between her banker father and this Idaho nephew. Capelton Belden lay on the ground, feet toward the fire, while the rest of the group perched on logs and flat stones. The two would like each other, although Peter Belden would probably disapprove of Cap's long brown hair tied with a leather thong at the nape of a strong neck. From the minute she and the others had stepped off the plane that morning in Wallace, Idaho, Trixie had been aware that both Brian and Mart were trying not to notice Cap's swinging ponytail.

Cap wore Indian moccasins. His leather jacket dangled fringes. Without appearing outlandish, Cap fitted the here and now. The here was a camp high in Idaho's mountains. The now was a starlit August Monday night.

Trixie was ecstatic over this sudden break in the end-of-summer routine on Crabapple Farm. Less than two days ago, she had been scalding and skinning tomatoes for canning, a job she loathed. And now she was almost the width of the continent away from the Hudson River valley. Bless Honey's father for his generosity! When Matt Wheeler had learned of his business conference in Seattle, he had filled the vacant seats of his company's plane with the Bob-Whites of the Glen, the club made up of Trixie and her friends.

It had not been difficult to persuade Miss Trask to accompany them. The manager of the Wheeler estate was eager to learn more about the Idaho wilderness. Because she so seldom interfered with their plans, Miss Trask was always the Bob-Whites' first choice for chaperon.

Dan Mangan was the only Bob-White who had not been able to fly west, due to his temporary job as counselor at an upstate New York boys' camp.

Recalling that Dan and Hallie had become good friends during Hallie's eastern visit, Trixie called across the circle, "Hallie, Dan said to tell you 'hi.' He wishes he could have come."

"Thanks, Trix. I was kind of hoping he could, too."

At the mention of a boy's name, Hallie's brothers glanced at each other, but they did not tease. Trixie liked that. In their shoes, Mart would have recited the entire balcony scene from *Romeo and Juliet.*

Knut shifted weight and stared upward at the sky-scraping pines. After a while he said, "Stars, hide your fires." His tone was as conversational as if he had said, "Please pass the butter."

"Jeepers," breathed Trixie, "did you make that up?"

"Nope," Knut answered good-naturedly.

"Shakespeare beat him to it," Jim guessed.

"Nothing wrong with quoting a little Shakespeare," said Hallie, staring proudly at Knut.

At thirteen, Hallie Belden was beautiful. Her bones were long and fragile-looking. Her braided, smooth hair was as dark as Brian's. She had eyes the color of ripe blackberries and brows that would never need tweezers. Trixie had no trouble imagining Hallie as a rajah's daughter in floating silks, but there she sat—in well-worn blue jeans, an old plaid shirt, and scuffed boots. Trixie doubted that she would ever be able to overcome a niggle-naggle of jealousy. She herself weighed a few more pounds than any of the other girls, and she wasn't as tall. It was hard to think of herself as pretty, when each time she faced Mart she saw herself—sandy curls, round blue eyes, and freckles. Mart was many things, but he wasn't *pretty!*

Something Brian said made Hallie laugh. The deep, gurgling chuckle caused others to smile with her. She clapped her hands, then made a welcoming gesture that included the Bob-Whites and Miss Trask. "I'm so glad you're here that I'm just bustin' buttons trying to think what to share with you first!"

"Something edible?" Mart suggested helpfully.

Cap looked astounded. "Wasn't that you who just ate three hot dogs in buns?" he asked.

Mart tried to sound deeply wounded. "My own cousin, mine host, actually counts the morsels with which I barely maintain this emaciated body!"

"You're about as emaciated as a hippo," Trixie snorted.

"Well, I'm just a little dry," Mart said hastily. "There's some watermelon in the creek that I just know—"

Knut started to rise but Hallie motioned her brother to sit down. "Later," she promised. "We'll have the melon later."

"We will if we beat that porcupine to it," Cap said.

"What porcupine?" Di squealed.

"Ssh!" Cap warned.

In the silence that fell, Trixie could hear the grumbling and chittering of a porcupine. She heard other sounds, too. A whistle and a snort.

"There's a deer close by," Knut whispered. "Something startled it."

"What's that bawling sound?" Trixie whispered back.

"Bear cub," Knut told her.

"That means its mother is hanging around, too?" Trixie asked, edging even closer to Knut.

"Or soon will be," Knut said.

There was another sound.

Cap seemed to float up into a sitting position. His brown eyes became as alert as those of a fox. Not a sound betrayed his own presence, but Trixie caught an exchange of glances between Cap and Knut.

A twig snapped. Again the bear cub squalled. To Trixie, that woods baby sounded scared.

The camp had been set up in a parklike glade beside Champion Creek where it tumbled down a steep, narrow gulch. Sounds were funneled to the campground as if through a megaphone: a series of grunts, barks, and wails . . . a sharp whistle . . . a coaxing *suka, suka.* Then, after a breathless wait, a long, drawn-out *agoouummm.*

"It's going away," Knut said.

"What was it?" asked Jim. "What animals do you have around here?"

Knut didn't seem to hear the first question. "Oh, the usual," he said. "Cougar, deer, elk, brown bear, skunk, whistling marmot."

"I thought a marmot was a kind of rodent," Trixie ventured.

"It is," Cap said.

"Well, that was an awfully big sound," Trixie declared.

"Maybe it was an awfully big rat," said Di nervously.

"Maybe," Cap said. He snapped a dry stick. The sound echoed like a gunshot.

Immediately the surrounding forest became so quiet that Trixie could hear the burble of water that swirled around large, white rocks in the dim half-light beyond the circle of firelight. No matter how hard she looked, she could see nothing but black-dark beyond those stones. Suddenly it seemed very important that she know exactly where she was at that very moment, where she would be when she put her head on her pillow, and where she would be when she woke up the next morning.

"Just where are we, anyway?" she asked finally. "Gleeps, we went around so many curves after we left Wallace this morning, I decided you were taking us to the moon."

Cap chortled. "We did, cousin. We took you to the Moon and kept right on going."

Trixie frowned.

Knut reached over to gather both her hands for a quick, reassuring squeeze. "The pass is called Moon," he explained. "There's a mountain named Moon, too, and a creek. Cap's just trying to rattle you."

"Like a birdbrain," Hallie added.

"We're in northern Idaho's St. Joe National Forest," Knut went on. "You may have seen the trail signs as we drove in this morning. Most of the northern half of Idaho is covered with the largest stand of virgin white pine remaining in the United States. This area is divided into five national forests. The Kaniksu and the Coeur d'Alene stretch from the Canadian border to the mining region. Next comes Joe, covering all that space between the Bitterroot Range on Montana's border to the wheatlands on the west. The mines are largely in the Coeur d'Alene

Mountains. The next mountain range south is called the St. Joe. The forest keeps marching south to cow country."

As Knut stood to point out the compass points in the sky, his shadow grew to monstrous proportions and moved crazily when the flames leaped. Trixie had a momentary vision of a prehistoric man claiming his territory. She sensed that these Idaho cousins' hearts were anchored in this rocky land just as firmly as her own family's roots were in Crabapple Farm and the Hudson River valley.

"All around us," Knut said quietly, "there are peaks that belong to eagles, and valleys where animals aren't afraid of men. There's mystery and treasure, adventure, danger, and quiet that stretches from earth to sky."

"That sounds like poetry," Miss Trask said.

"And I'll bet it isn't Shakespeare," added Honey.

"It isn't," Knut admitted. "Thank you."

"Any of you guys smoke?" Cap asked.

"No" was the prompt reply from both girls and boys.

"Good," Cap said. "Welcome to Joe Country."

After Knut sat down again, Trixie said, "Pinch me, somebody! I must be dreaming. I don't have to feed those stupid hens when I wake up tomorrow!" She joined the chuckle at her expense. Nobody could accuse Trixie Belden of enjoying chores. Mystery was her interest, first, last, and always—and, oh, this Joe Country must hold a thousand unsolved mysteries. Why else was the blond fuzz standing up on her bare forearms?

At that moment, an eerie cry that originated at the head of the canyon hit unseen cliffs and echoed endlessly: *fleep . . . fleeoweep-p-p-p!*

Cap jumped up and began feeding the fire with reckless haste.

"You're using the morning kindling," Hallie objected.

"So what?" Cap shot back.

"Don't be a birdbrain!"

"Look, I cut this. I can split more." Fire gobbled the dry pitch Cap threw. Light increased in intensity, and so did Cap's effort.

Without understanding why, Mart, Brian, and Jim began to throw on all the dry, small wood scraps they could find in the circle of light. Knut moved to the outer edge of the lighted area and stared up the dark slot of the canyon.

Trixie hunched alone on the log Knut and Jim had deserted. She was sure she would hear that cry again.

She did. This time it came from some spot just beyond those white rocks. When she pulled in her breath to keep from screaming, she choked on the nauseating smell-taste of rotten fish and dead field mice.

Lonely Vigil • 2

A COUGAR SCREECHED at the same time that Hallie choked, "What is that gosh-awful smell?"

"A carcass," Knut said.

"A bee trap," Cap corrected him quickly.

Again Trixie saw her cousins having an eye conversation.

Along with the rest of the campers, the usually unflappable Miss Trask was openly gagging. "Well, which is it?" she asked.

Knut hesitated, then said, "Cap's usually right about things in the woods. Yes, it's a bee trap."

"We've been here most of the day setting up

camp," Hallie said flatly. "I didn't see another car nearby. I didn't hear another car. Not even a motorcycle. So who set a bee trap?"

Knut adjusted his glasses and waited for Cap to speak.

Cap strolled to the outer edge of the fire circle. "A fisherman, maybe, while he cleaned his trout. Or another camper."

"Somebody who's already pulled out," Knut agreed.

Trixie didn't have brothers of her own for nothing. Knut and Cap were building an explanation out of thin air. They didn't know any more than she did what had caused that fetid odor.

Hallie held her nose and declared, "They'd better change recipes."

"Or their good neighbor policy," Brian said with a hollow laugh.

"Why would anybody want to trap a bee?" Di asked. "I thought they were good for making honey and leaving it in trees for bears to eat."

Knut's surprised chuckle broke the tension. "That's one way to look at it, Di, but when you're trying to clean fish or cook, yellow jackets can get pretty pesky. Woodsmen get some protection when they hang a fine-meshed wire basket several feet away from where they're working. They smear stale fish—usually just the heads—with cooking fat and anything else they can find that will turn rancid in the sun. They put the mess in the basket and let nature take its course. Yellow jackets are scavengers. They go for the rotten food and leave the fishermen in peace."

Di wrinkled her nose with distaste.

Cap's brown ponytail swung as he quit his prowling and sat beside her. "Never mind," he said. "We'll take care of it in the morning."

The wind changed and soon it was possible to breathe freely. Still, Trixie sensed restlessness in the forest. A great owl swooped low through the clearing. Coyotes argued, came to some agreement, and moved on. Once she thought she heard that cranky bear cub.

Trixie agreed with the theory that nothing was in the woods at night that wasn't there in broad daylight. But that was more comforting when she was in the Wheeler game preserve, way back home on the Hudson River. This was the vast Joe country in Idaho. Who knew what might be watching every move she made? Hugging herself, Trixie hunched toward the fire.

"Are you cold?" Knut asked. "Shall I bring an extra sweater? Our temperature drops pretty low after sundown."

"No, thanks, Knut," Trixie answered quickly. "I just thought about home and a—a goose walked over my grave!"

"How appropriate!" Mart exclaimed. "It has come often to my attention that warm-blooded vertebrate animals characterized by oviparous generation and covered by an epidermal growth are prone to gather in companies. Therefore, a web-footed anserine fowl would seek out its kind, namely one Beatrix Belden, aged fourteen, familiarly known as Trixie, the co-president of this otherwise intelligent band of youth called the Bob-Whites of the Glen." Mart's swooping right hand included Di, Jim, Honey, Brian, and Trixie.

His sister stopped hugging herself. "Heaven—with help from the dictionary—only knows, but I do believe you're insulting me!"

Jim Frayne sprawled comfortably at Trixie's right. "If he is, he really got carried away and labeled all of us geese, himself included. That is, unless Mart has recently resigned from the Bob-Whites. As the other co-president, I'd be happy to entertain a motion that his resignation be accepted without further ado!"

"I second the motion!" Hallie whooped. She waved a hand, which Mart promptly captured and pulled down.

Where Mart Belden was concerned, Di Lynch would listen to no criticism. "You can't do that, Hallie," she objected prettily. "Nobody made a motion for you to second."

"I'll be glad to oblige," Brian put in.

Mart smote his brow. "Betrayed first by my own tongue and then by my brother's."

Hallie clapped her hands and grinned as she told her own brothers, "See? I told you it was fun being a Bob-White!"

"We're not members," Knut said.

"You are now," Jim said. "All in favor of accepting Hallie, Cap, and Knut as honorary new members, say 'aye.' "

"Aye!" shouted the visiting New Yorkers.

"Now what do we do?" Cap asked. "Wear feathers in our hair?"

"Be serious!" Trixie begged. "It's—well, it's an honor to belong to the Bob-Whites of the Glen. We're pledged to help each other or anybody else in need, and we're semi-secret—we don't go around bragging about the good deeds we do."

"Our signal is the bob-white call," added Honey, "and we use it only when we really need help." She pursed her lips and gave the *bob, bob-white* call in a clear, sweet whistle.

"That's better than *fleep, fleeoweep.*" Softly

Cap whistled the unbearably lonely cry that had echoed through the canyon a short while ago.

"H-Have y-you heard that scream before tonight?" Trixie asked.

Cap dug a moccasin heel into the pine needle ground cover. After a long silence, he looked up. "A few times" was all he would say.

"What about you, Knut, and you, Hallie?" Trixie demanded.

"No," Knut said. "But Cap told me about it."

"Anybody care to strain a tonsil to let us in on the scary secret?" Hallie inquired.

"Never mind, Hallie," Cap said. "He's gone now."

"He?" Mart asked alertly. "How do you know it's a he?"

"I don't," Cap said. "But it's over seven feet tall and—"

"Cool it, Cap," Knut said quietly.

Cap rose quickly and asked, "Who wants to help me serve the watermelon?"

"Allow me!" Mart volunteered.

The cousins marched off to the stream to lift two huge watermelons from the icy water. Hallie ran for a big metal dishpan. She set it on the long portable camp table. Cap unsheathed the hunting knife strapped to his wide belt. When he cut the first melon, it popped like a rifle shot.

"Oh, yum!" Di squealed. She jumped up to help Mart dole out the dripping, sweet treat.

While Mart pretended to weigh and measure the slices to be sure they were equal, Trixie concentrated on every small sound that came out of the dark. What was there in this forest that stood over seven feet tall? A bear might stretch to that height when it stood. A deer didn't make that noise. What else . . . ? She stared at her watermelon without really seeing it.

"I know that watermelon probably isn't a goose's favorite food," Mart was saying patiently, "but—"

Trixie ignored him. "How tall is a moose?" she asked Knut.

"Well over seven feet at the shoulder," he told her.

"What kind of a sound does he make?"

"He bellows. Have you heard an elephant at a circus? The sound is similar." Knut realized the intent behind her questions and added, "Don't worry about it, Trixie. Nobody's reported an incident so far."

Knut turned his attention to Miss Trask, who wanted to know how to recognize the famous Idaho white pine. Trixie heard Knut explain, "Its needles, or leaves, are in clusters of five, and the tree grows straight. It can reach a height of two hundred feet."

No incident so far, Trixie mused. *What an odd thing to say! What kind of incident? And where would one be reported? Cap didn't build that fire to such height and brightness to scare off a moose!*

When the last juicy bite of watermelon had been eaten, Cap collected the rinds and heaped them in the dishpan. "No need to bury them. The porcupines will polish off this treat by morning. I'll dump them down the creek, so we won't have the varmints wandering through camp all night."

"If you run across that bee trap, take care of it, will you, Cap?" Hallie asked.

Cap looked startled, then he mumbled, "Oh, sure." He strode into the dark, carrying the load of rinds.

"Hey, wait for me!" Mart scrambled up to follow.

Trixie watched them go, aware of an unexpected likeness they shared. Even though Mart was noisy and Cap quiet, Mart the performer and Cap the audience, Mart conservative in taste while Cap chose his own style, both shared a love of the earth itself. Both felt a oneness with earth's creatures and products. She wondered if

Cap also shared the memory that allowed Mart to spout dictionaries at will and to report accurately all the odd bits of information that caught his attention.

She turned to ask Knut, "Does Cap read a lot?"

"Depends on what you mean by 'a lot.' " Knut smiled with a duplicate of Brian's smile. "Cap's English teacher would say he never cracks a book, but she'd be wrong. He hangs around the forestry lookout and memorizes all the government pamphlets."

"Then Cap knows all that goes on in the woods?" Trixie persisted.

"Cap knows," Knut said soberly. He turned away to listen intently.

Once again, there came a *suka*, *suka*, *suka*, little more than a whisper far downstream.

Trixie sighed deeply and realized she had been holding her breath while she waited for the reappearance of Cap and Mart. A small grunt from Knut let her know that he, too, was relieved when the young men returned, swinging the dishpan between them and chanting the nursery rhyme "Jack and Jill." Trixie fervently wished they had not chosen to repeat that particular rhyme at this particular instant. Both Jack and Jill had fallen down that hill of theirs.

Miss Trask stood up and brushed the bark from her squeaky new blue jeans. "Bedtime, my friends," she announced. "Now, tell me, how do we dispose of the fire?"

"Knut and I will take care of it, Miss Trask," Cap said quickly, "if the rest of the fellows will help us carry water."

Soon full pails of water ringed the fire, although none was dumped on the deep bed of coals. Trixie overheard Cap ask, in an aside to Knut, "Before or after two?"

Trixie's bump of curiosity tingled like a jarred crazy bone. Her cousins were not planning to put out the fire. They were standing guard!

Was that usual?

Honey shared Trixie's small tent, and Di and Hallie were close neighbors. The entries to their tents faced each other and were near enough to be within hand-clasping distance.

"Wanna gab and giggle?" Hallie invited her guests.

Di and Honey agreed with delight, but Trixie was not in the mood—not when she could see Knut take up his lonely vigil, armed only with a flashlight.

Sasquatch! • 3

SEVERAL TIMES DURING THE NIGHT Trixie awoke, unused to being confined within a sleeping bag.

Once Honey roused at the same time. "Don't your cousins ever sleep?" she murmured. "Or do they wait till winter and hibernate like bears?"

Trixie forced a giggle.

Long after Honey slept again, Trixie propped her curly head on a hand to watch the shifting light of the campfire. She knew when it was two o'clock, because Cap quietly joined Knut. They spoke softly while Cap buttoned himself snugly into his jacket. Cap wasn't as tall or as heavy as Knut, but somehow Trixie felt safer when the young mountainman, with his moccasined feet and dangling fringes, stretched out on the ground beside the fire. Cap was one with the forest itself.

She heard Knut say, "If you need me, Capelton, whistle."

"Okay, Knutson. I will."

Trixie found their unexpected formality oddly comforting. It was nice to know that Knut and Cap Belden respected each other, even if she didn't know why they were keeping watch. She realized that Knut had thrown a red herring across her trail by describing the height of a moose. So what if it was seven feet tall at the point of the shoulder? What was there in this camp to attract a moose? Besides, no moose could have made the sounds they had heard. As Trixie finally fell asleep, she was still trying to decide what animal *could* have made those sounds.

Everyone said that Trixie's middle name might as well have been "Curiosity." It was her need to understand the mysterious that had led her and Honey to make plans for the Belden-Wheeler Detective Agency. They had already solved a number of puzzling mysteries in their home area of Sleepyside-on-the-Hudson. They had gone farther afield several times, gaining widespread publicity for their work. Those mysteries had involved stolen goods, lost wills, mistaken identity, and even a lost baby. Not once had they faced a mystery whose clues were a cry in the night and an odor.

Still restless from the excitement of the flight across the continent, Trixie stirred when the dawn song of birds greeted the new day. She yawned deeply. Gasping, she sat up in her bedroll, her hand over her mouth.

Fish! There it was again—that smell so fetid she could have retched!

A faint clicking sound made her look to see if Cap was still on guard.

As if in slow-motion, Cap drew up his knees until they almost touched his chest. He began to rise, inch by inch, like a mushroom pushing its body into air. Oh, so slowly, an arm reached toward the fire. Cap withdrew a long brand that had been smoldering within reach of his right hand.

Trixie oozed from her sleeping bag and put a bare foot on the cold canvas floor. First she'd awaken Honey, then Hallie and Di, then Miss Trask. The boys—could she reach them in time?

Just as Trixie stretched out her hand to touch Honey, common sense gained control. Cap wasn't making a sound. *If Cap thought people should be roused, he'd yell, wouldn't he?*

Trixie crept to the tent opening to see what Cap saw. She could make out nothing . . . except that every boulder, every bush, every stump or fallen log had taken on some fantastic bestial shape in the half-light. Then she saw it!

But what *was* it? Trixie went rigid with fear.

A very tall *thing* stood what seemed like only a few feet from Cap. Arms dangled past its knees. Its head and shoulders were joined like grotesque snowballs pushed together to make a snowman. Covered with fur from head to toe, it stood upright like a man and exuded that choking odor of dead fish and meadow mice.

Even in the midst of her terror, Trixie thought to herself, *So this is Cap's bee trap!*

Then the monster whined. The sound was like a question. Suddenly Cap brandished his firebrand so violently that fire flared into life. The monster stepped backward. Though it was huge, Trixie did not hear one crackle of a twig snapped under its feet.

Was this what Knut had meant by an "incident"? What should she *do?* Trixie pushed all her knuckles against her teeth.

Cap looked pitifully small and vulnerable beside this grossly huge forest monster. For a long instant, the two eyed each other across the hot ashes. The monster clicked its teeth, shifted its weight uncertainly, then disappeared in the wink of an eye. Only the odor that lingered behind was proof to Trixie that she had not dreamed a nightmare.

Cap pushed his firebrand back into the hot ashes. He looked so shaken that Trixie left her tent on the run.

"C-Cap!" she gasped. "Wh-What *was* it?"

"The sasquatch," he said.

"The *what?*"

Cap seemed to see Trixie for the first time. Roughly he told her, "Go get your boots. You'll freeze to death."

Trixie hopped on flinching, tender feet back to her tent and put on her boots. Realizing how ridiculously she was dressed, she snatched up the blanket that covered her bedroll. Snugly wrapped, she went back to Cap. "What's a sasquatch?" she demanded unceremoniously.

Cap didn't answer immediately. "You saw it, didn't you?" he asked finally.

Asked a pointblank question, Trixie hesitated. "Why—" She had to stand very close to Cap just to see his features clearly in the early morning light. Even that stump over by Miss Trask's tent looked like a bear. "I—I think so," she said.

Cap pushed his fingertips against his eyes. "So, I wasn't dreaming."

Trixie recalled the eye conversations between Cap and Knut. "Have you seen it before?" she persisted.

"No, but I've heard it several times. I've smelled it, and I've run across its tracks. But this is my first sighting."

"Will it come back?" Trixie asked soberly.

"Probably not. It's a night feeder, and night will soon be gone. Luckily, this was a friendly encounter."

"Jeepers, you call that friendly?"

"Well, it didn't harm us, did it?" Cap stirred the coals to life. "We'll need a breakfast fire," he murmured.

"Breakfast," Trixie repeated, lost in a reconstruction of the strange encounter. "Cap, what *is* a sasquatch?"

Cap shrugged. "It's a primate, or mammal, of some kind. It lives in the high country. In Asia they call it yeti or Abominable Snowman. Over here we call it sasquatch or bigfoot."

"I've heard about the Snowman," Trixie said, "but I always thought it was some kind of gimmick they made up to get people to go to the Himalayas. You know, like going to Scotland to see the Loch Ness Monster."

Cap looked amused.

Trixie's cheeks warmed. "Or a legend, like our Rip Van Winkle back home."

Cap jabbed the fire with his stick. "Pretty stinky legend, wouldn't you say?" Then he faced Trixie. "We aren't the first ones to see the sasquatch, and we won't be the last. There've been hundreds of recent sightings. Seeing it in the Joe country is what shakes me. I never dreamed I'd see it so far inland!" Cap shook his head to clear away cobwebs of sleeplessness and tension. "To be honest, Trixie, I never dreamed I'd ever see one, period."

"Maybe that's it—we dreamed it," Trixie said hopefully. As light poured into the campground, her dawn-terror was fading.

"Some dream," Cap sniffed. "It *was* sort of wonderful, though, wasn't it? Now I know how the scientists feel when they discover something a zillion years old."

"Sure, but those things get put in museums. This thing was right here—alive and well!" Trixie felt dizzy. "Maybe—maybe what we saw was an ape."

"Too little."

"How about a gorilla? He could have escaped from a zoo or a circus train. Have there been any circus accidents in the Northwest recently?"

Trixie knew she was grasping at straws, but she felt so uncomfortable with the knowledge that a monster, neither man nor beast, had planted its feet on this very soil.

"The tracks will tell the story," Cap said shortly. He shaded his tired eyes from the sun-rays that dropped through tall white pines. "It's light enough—come on."

Cap left the fire pit, stooping low to look at the ground. Clutching her blanket and clumping in her unlaced boots, Trixie followed. Cap made three widening circles before he found the first clear track.

Cap whistled. "Trix, look at the size of it!"

"I'm looking," she whispered. "How many hands is it?"

"Hands?" Cap whispered back.

"You know, like measuring horses. A palm is about four inches."

"Oh, sure." Quickly Cap moved hand over hand. He sat back on his heels. "That print is at least eighteen inches."

"Yipes!" Trixie gasped.

"Let's see where it went." Noticing Trixie's blanket, Cap added, "I'll wait till you dress."

"Oh, jeepers, please do!"

Cap's long legs carried him around the circle to Knut's pup tent before Trixie reached her own. Cap whistled sharply.

At once Knut answered, "Cap?"

"On the double," Cap ordered. "I'll get the other fellows."

"Shall I wake the girls?" Trixie called.

"Might as well," Cap answered. "Why should they sleep when we're awake?"

Within minutes, the glade echoed with mumbles, yawns, and shouts. Miss Trask put her gray head through her tent door to inquire, "Is this the customary hour to rise?"

Tucking in the tail of her flannel shirt, Hallie whooped, "It's daylight in the swamp!"

First awake, Trixie was the last of the girls to reappear at the campfire, fully clothed, teeth brushed, and hair combed. She looked at Cap and raised her brows.

"I didn't tell them," he answered.

"Tell us what?" Di wanted to know.

"We had a visitor," Cap began.

Hallie wrinkled her nose. "Ugh, I can still smell that pesky bee trap. Did your visitor bring it with him?"

"Kind of," Cap said.

"In fact, he *was* the bee trap," Trixie added.

"Elucidate!" Mart ordered.

"I'll do better than that," Cap answered. "I'll show you." He led the way to the footprint.

Brian squatted to study the giant print. Toes all of a size and almost squared off had dug a deep ridge in the earth. Brian muttered about the flattened arch and the wide heel. He was completely puzzled by the double ball to the foot.

"That print has three times the surface area of a man's foot!" Brian declared. "What—" he cleared his throat—"made it?"

"The sasquatch," Trixie said.

"Oh, Trixie, that's just a myth," said her big brother.

"Don't be too sure," Trixie warned soberly.

Only One Road • 4

DI'S VIOLET EYES grew wide and disturbed. "I don't know what you're talking about, and I'm pretty sure I don't want to!"

"I think I know," said Miss Trask, "but I must say I'd always put sasquatches in the same category as goblins and ghosts. Not that this footprint isn't convincing, but—" Miss Trask put an arm across Di's shaking shoulders and drew her toward the supply chests in the kitchen area. Over her shoulder she called, "We can discuss the problem better when we've been fed properly." As if marshaling troops, Miss Trask assigned tasks in a cheerful, efficient voice.

Trixie heard Cap mutter to Knut, "I thought we left Ollie at home." Trixie knew that Ollie was their maid.

"You'll love Miss Trask when you get to know her," Trixie promised them. "How would *you* like to be wakened from a sound sleep at sunup to be told a—a *sasquatch* had just left camp? Anyway, she does have the right idea—about food, I mean."

"I'm starving," Cap declared. "And I'll bet anything Mart is."

"If you say so, I guess I am," said Mart as he caught up to them. "So what am I, and what's my job?"

Trixie realized that Mart hadn't heard Miss Trask. She also knew that Cap had been assigned to dishwashing, so she told Mart, "You're a hungry dishwasher." Then she hurried off to set the table.

"I knew I'd be sorry I asked," Mart muttered.

Brown eyes dancing, Cap joined Trixie. In a low voice he asked, "What was that all about?"

"I have a good memory when it comes to brothers calling me a goose," Trixie said, lifting her chin. "Oh, by the way, Mart was water carrier, so I guess you're it."

"Good," Cap said. "I want to look for more tracks before they get messed up."

Trixie raced around the folding table, scattering knives, forks, and spoons. "Please wait for me! I'm the detective in this family!"

"So I've heard," Cap said admiringly. He picked up a stack of enameled mugs and followed Trixie's example. "There, that should do it."

Trixie giggled. "Miss Trask won't give us *A* for effort. Let's go!"

With pails swinging, Cap and Trixie set off down a trail that one day's use had marked from campground to creek.

"The earth's surface is fragile," Cap said. "By the time we've left here, we'll have changed the whole growth schedule of all the plants we're walking on."

Anxiously Trixie looked at the earth. She tried to put her boot soles on the bare earth, not on the delicate-looking white goatsbeard and the shiny-leafed pipsissewa.

"Don't walk on the bare spots," Cap warned. "That's where we may find a print."

"You're hard to please," Trixie commented, following him downstream in a soundless, elbow-pumping lope.

A couple of hundred yards from the fire pit, ants worked on tiny melon scraps that larger animals had missed.

Cap read tracks as if scanning the pages of a

book. "A skunk. Two porkies."

"How do you know there were two porcupines?" Trixie asked. "One could have moved around a lot."

"Track sizes," Cap explained. "Probably mother and young." He whistled. "What have we here?"

Trixie stood beside Cap and stared down at a duplicate of the enormous track left by the fire pit.

"It l-likes people food," Trixie gulped.

"Now I wish we had buried those rinds," said Cap.

Trixie tried to rub down chill bumps of apprehension. "I always feel my skin prickle when I run across something I don't understand," she confessed.

"Me, too. But we have a big problem now—how to avoid a panic."

"Gleeps, you're right," said Trixie. "How shall we start?"

"With breakfast under our belts," Cap said firmly.

Minutes later, Trixie and Cap had joined the others and were wolfing down juicy pink ham and great dollops of scrambled eggs and fried cornmeal mush. It wasn't long before the conversation turned to the sasquatch.

"Cap, did you really see him?" asked Brian. "Or did you just—"

"Saw him," Cap said firmly. "Smelled him. Heard him."

"You forgot tasted." Trixie wrinkled her nose at the memory of the rank, oily odor.

"Haven't you been reading about the sasquatch sightings?" Knut asked Brian.

"Not much," Brian admitted.

Knut frowned. "You can think the beast is a myth if you like, but Cap and Trix didn't model a footprint to give us a thrill. Nor have dozens of other citizens. Our own state university has put out a scientific pamphlet of facts and theories related to the sasquatch. For example, a crippled one has been tracked in the vicinity of Spokane, Washington. Now, as the crow flies, that's no more than seventy-five miles from here. Of course, this fellow can't fly, but it has unusually long, strong legs. It could cover a lot of miles in a short time if it had to."

"Wasn't there a bogus sighting in California?" asked Mart.

"More than one," Cap agreed. "Publicity hounds always get into the act."

"Our Northwest anthropologists are asking for all the information they can get," Knut went on. "The problem is, they don't know what to do with the information they already have. People have heard monster stories all their lives. Even if they make some kind of contact with the sasquatch, they're embarrassed to come forward and say so. Who wants to be called a crackpot?"

"Well, what are the facts?" asked Miss Trask.

"Anthropologists are tabulating the locations and dates of footprints and fur tufts that are found," said Knut. "They're interviewing people who've made sightings. Oregon's taken the first step in trying to protect the species. They've passed a law that forbids shooting the sasquatch. They're hoping to capture a live animal, although any body, alive or dead, would be final proof of existence."

"What does it eat?" Di asked anxiously.

"Some say vegetable matter," Cap answered, "but it'll take anything it can get. I'm prepared to state that it likes melon."

Miss Trask looked thoughtful. "I can't say I'm fully convinced that the creature exists. In any case, Diana, I'm sure that Knut and Cap will do a fine job of looking out for us."

An uncomfortable silence developed. Then Cap said, "My ears seldom lie, and I've heard three new sounds recently." Eerily he imitated the cries: *suka, suka, suka . . . agoouummm . . .*

fleep, fleeoweep! Hearing that yelp again made the hairs prickle on Trixie's arms.

"From reading and from talking with hunters, I've learned that bigfoot makes a number of sounds," Cap went on. "It grunts, whinnies, cackles, wails, and cries. It even shrills like a very large pine squirrel. This spring, a lineman for the telephone company told of seeing huge footprints in the snow up on Champion. That's northeast." Cap jerked a thumb in the general direction of the peak.

"Is that a major peak?" Jim asked.

"About average," said Cap. "Over six thousand feet."

"Mount Everest is almost equal to five Champion Peaks stacked like pancakes," added Knut. "Asia's Abominable Snowman lives pretty close to the sky."

Just then, conversation was disrupted by a troop of boy campers marching into camp, jittery with excitement.

Their leader thrust out a hand as he strode forward. "I'm Herb Galloway from Walla Walla." His manner was hearty, but his eyes were watching shadows in the forest.

"Jim Frayne, New York State," said Jim, who was closest.

"New York, you say? Long way from home.

I'll wager you didn't plan to turn right around and go back where it's safe." The man laughed unnaturally loudly.

"Go back?" Di repeated. "We just got here."

Mr. Galloway straightened, then crossed his arms against his khaki shirt. "Folks, it is my duty to warn you that a dangerous beast is feeding in this valley. I'd advise you to pack up and get out of here before sundown."

"Why?" Trixie asked. "Was somebody hurt?"

"I'm happy to report the answer is negative." Herb Galloway's eyes slid past Trixie's face and continued their shadow-searching.

The troop's smallest boy piped, "Haven't we done our duty, Mr. Galloway? We've warned 'em, so let's go!"

Abruptly, almost sharply, Mart asked Galloway, "Isn't your action apt to cause a panic?"

"A panic?" Trixie repeated. "Oh, Cap—"

Cap faced the man from Walla Walla. "Someone's going to get trigger-happy and shoot the sasquatch."

"What's one sasquatch more or less if human lives are saved?" Herb shot back. "Anyway, I didn't mention the sasquatch, did I? Now, you take my advice, folks. Get a move on." Herb Galloway marched around the table to shake hands with Miss Trask before leading his band of small boys on its rescue mission.

When he had disappeared, Miss Trask said briskly, "How very kind of him. How soon are we prepared to take his advice?"

Silently the Bob-Whites searched each other's faces.

Hotly Hallie declared, "I don't know about the rest of you, but I'm not leaving without at least warning old Tank that he might be in for a surprise!"

"Who's Tank?" Di asked.

"He's an old prospector we've known all our lives," Knut told her. "He used to work for Dad. His real name is Anders Anderson, and he has a one-man operation at the head of this canyon." Knut nodded at the deep slot in the mountain.

Trixie felt her heart skip a beat. Hadn't she first heard that strange cry from the head of this very canyon? If somebody lived up there, how could Cap be so sure there had been no unhappy "incident"? Trixie glanced up to see Hallie's black eyes staring into her own.

Cap poured a second mug of orange juice and explained, "Tank has lived alone so long he doesn't really know how to keep a conversation going. He always greets you with 'Ay tank de tistles be tick dis year." So we call him Tank. He doesn't mind."

As Cap went on, it was obvious that Tank was someone the Idaho Beldens were enormously fond of. "He has a placer, or gravel, mine in a dry creek bed that forks off from our creek. He has a tight cabin and plants a few spuds, carrots, cabbage, and stuff like that. He's panned for gold in cold water so long that he's got 'rheumatiz.' It's hard for him to get across the saddle to town, so Knut and I kind of look out for him."

"There you go again," Di complained. "What's a saddle? I know you're not talking about horses. Sometimes I think that Idaho isn't just a state—it's a language!"

"A saddle is a mountain ridge," Knut said, smiling at Di's bewilderment. "Remember when we came over the Moon? That's the pass over the saddle. To get back to town, everybody has to go over the saddle. There's only one road."

"Oh!" Di's eyes were troubled.

"What's your problem?" Hallie drawled.

"It's just that—what if the sas—the you-know-what sits on that saddle?"

Tank • 5

UNEASINESS SILENCED the group as it considered the possibility that the sasquatch might be lurking on the only road leading directly from the national forest to the closest towns of the mining region.

Then Hallie jumped up from the breakfast table. "The sasquatch may be many things, but it can't be in two places at the same time. I'm going to take my chances that old 'squatch *is* sitting on that saddle. *I'm* going to Tank's cabin if I have to go alone!"

Cheeks blazing red, Hallie gathered up her place setting and went over to the huge metal dishpan. There she sloshed her own dishes and silver in hot suds, dipped them into a second pan of boiling water, and tilted them in a rack. "There, I'm ready. Who's going with me?"

"You know we're all going," Mart said gruffly. "Right, Miss Trask?"

"I suppose so," Miss Trask agreed after a moment's hesitation.

"Not till this mess is cleaned up," Cap ordered. "Not one crumb of food is to be left out to draw bears."

While everyone cleared away all traces of food, closed tents, and locked hasps on storage chests, Trixie tried to keep track of sounds, shadows, and odors. Until Di dropped an owl's feather on the coals that Cap was dousing with water, the clean smell of sun-warmed pine needles was all that filled the campground.

"Brian, suppose you take over the foot-check while I fill canteens," called Cap.

Brian made sure that everyone's soft, clean socks were smooth, with boots firmly but not too tightly laced. "Extra socks in your pocket?" Cap asked as he handed each person a canteen of cold fresh water.

Within minutes, camp was out of sight. Birds had fed early and were silent, but other small animals were going about their business.

Honey, who was Trixie's trail buddy, commented, "None of the animals seems to be nervous. I don't think I'm going to manufacture a lot of adrenaline I'm not going to use."

"You sound like Mart," Trixie giggled, "but I think I know what you mean." From that moment, Trixie enjoyed the climb up the canyon, reserving only a small, alert part of her mind to stand guard. With Honey, she sang a marching song Honey had learned at camp when much younger.

Then, in a rich contralto voice, Hallie followed it with a spirited miner's song.

Next, Knut sang, in a strong, pleasant tenor: "Sweetly sings the donkey, at the break of day. If you do not feed him, this is what he'll say. . . ."

With much gusto, Cap, Mart, Brian, and Jim roared, "Hee-haw, hee-haw, hee-haw, hee-haw, hee-haw!" Their feet thumped the steep trail, beating the rhythm.

"Distances sure are deceiving in Idaho," Di complained good-naturedly a little later when she dropped back to join Honey and Trixie for a while.

"I think it's just that we're used to riding our horses back at home," Honey told her. "But I'm beginning to wonder if the head of this canyon was just an illusion when we saw it back at our camp. We've been hiking almost two hours now."

Just when Trixie was sure she couldn't climb another yard, quite unexpectedly the trail leveled. Trees were not so tall or so closely spaced. The August sun beat down on a flat area.

"Tank, hey, Tank!" roared Knut, Cap, and Hallie.

"Yah, sure!" The happy response came from the left.

Trixie had not expected a hermit miner to be over six feet tall, thin as a sapling, and dressed in white. Even his bald head glowed whitely above a freshly shaven pink face.

Tank was chopping weeds that grew in the queerest garden Trixie had ever seen. In cleared spaces among huckleberry bushes and Indian-paint brush, Tank had disturbed the earth just enough to insert a few seeds. In a helter-skelter way, he grew potatoes, onions, carrots, beans, and cabbages. The watering system was primitive but adequate—two pails and a dipper. Damp areas showed where he had dribbled water on the plants that needed it.

Tank placed both hands on the end of his upright hoe handle. When he leaned his chin on his hands, his long body bent like a bow. He examined space from earth to sky. Then he said slowly and carefully, "Ay tank de tistles be tick dis year. Yah?"

"Yah!" whooped Knut, Cap, and Hallie. They rushed forward to hug him.

Knut drew Trixie, Brian, and Mart forward. "These are our cousins from New York State." Next he introduced Miss Trask, Di, Honey, and Jim.

"How've you been, Tank?" asked Cap. "Do you need anything?"

"Now that ya put me in mind of it, Cap, ay could use some pep'mint drops 'n' a slab of hawg." Bright blue eyes swept over the group. "You young'uns et yet? Ma'am, could ay pull up a fresh drink fer ya?"

Miss Trask's face showed only momentary confusion. "Thank you, Mr. Anderson. I must confess I drank all my water on the climb up the mountain."

"Come on in where it's shady and cool," Tank invited.

Everyone entered the fenced area around a small house built of rough-hewn logs and mountain stone. The trees around it kept it cool in summer and snug in winter.

"Gimme a minute and ay'll cool ya off fine." Tank disappeared into the cabin, with Hallie at his heels.

"Where does he get water on a mountaintop?" Di asked.

Before Mart could launch into a many-syllabled reply, Cap answered, "Tank boxed in a spring. He has a pump."

Hallie came out of Tank's house, balancing a dishpan filled with tin cups and a plate of the biggest cookies Trixie had ever seen. Tank carried the pail of water. He walked past the group to disappear behind a low door that seemed to be fitted into the mountain itself.

When he came out, he said, "Vet yer vistles!"

Miss Trask was first to be served. "My word, Mr. Anderson. Lemonade?"

"With ice," Honey said wonderingly. "Oh, Mr. Anderson, you shouldn't waste your ice and lemons on us. I know how hard it must be to bring ice all the way over Moon Pass and up that steep trail."

Tank's laughter boomed. "Ay had half a year to fill my ice cave. Ve got yust three seasons in the Yoe country. Yune—"

"Yuly and Vinter!" Hallie finished with a shout.

"Vant to see how ay keep my wittles fresh?" Tank put a hand on one hip as he loped back to the ice cave. "Oh, this rheumatiz. Ain't been vorking much dis veek, but ay got it yust the same."

"Tank, you know darned well you don't have

to work that claim if you don't want to," Knut scolded good-naturedly. "You've got enough dust stored to last you the rest of your life."

"Yah, sure," Tank agreed. "But ay like to be sure ay can even up me owing's vhile ay still can."

Tank opened the door of his cave. Everyone crowded close to peer at chunks of ice packed in pine needles. Venison, bear meat, and several ducks hung from a rack. Brook trout lay frozen in ice. A few vegetables from last year's garden were carefully stored on a slotted bench that allowed moisture to drain away.

"You certainly aren't going to starve, sir," Jim said.

"I admire your ability to cope with the wilderness, Mr. Anderson," added Mart.

"Ay ain't aiming to skimp on me wittles," Tank answered. "Call me Tank. Dese young scalavags've been doing that for so long ay start peering about for me father when ya say 'Mr. Anderson.' "

When they walked back to the yard to enjoy their lemonade and cookies, Trixie heard Tank tell Knut, "It's gettin' hard for me to traipse across that saddle to town. Vith all yer company, ya sure ya don't mind toting me dust an' picking up a few t'ings?"

"Mind?" Knut slapped Tank's shoulder affectionately. "I'd mind if you *didn't* let me do it for you. We've got it planned to break the monotony of camp life with a drive-in movie sometime this weekend, anyway."

Tank nudged Knut's ribs. "And ay tank ya vant to see that Gloria, huh?"

"That, too," Knut said, laughing. "If I don't show up Friday night, she'll be dating some other guy!"

"Not vith you around," Tank declared.

Cap and Knut upended chunks of logs for extra chairs, and Tank fetched a chair from the cabin for Miss Trask. Its legs were hand-carved of cedar, the back was contrived of moose antlers, and the seat was a sheet of deerskin.

"This is a museum piece," said Miss Trask with delight. "Priceless."

"So are the cookies," Honey said.

"Museum pieces?" Brian teased.

"No, silly; priceless. Tank, how do you make them?"

"Ay dump oats and bear grease and molasses into my crock. Then ay chunk 'em all together vith flour and dried huckleberries and some leavening. Alvays it comes out cookies."

"Bear grease?" Di looked at her saucer-sized cookie and gulped.

"If *you* don't like it—" Mart began.

"I like it!" Di exclaimed hastily and began munching.

When the last cookie was eaten, Cap asked casually, "Had any company lately, Tank?"

"Company? Do ya count fishermen and kids on noisy trail bikes? Yah, sure. Some."

"Well, how about—" Cap chewed ice and stared into space—"night company?"

Tank grinned broadly. "There's Old Gray—he yells every night till all the coyotes over Park Crick vay, they take up that rackety song. Loverly 'n' me, ve listen. Yah, that's company for us. Night company."

Knut explained that Loverly was Tank's pet skunk.

Cap kept right on chewing ice, without looking at Tank.

"Ya vant to hear about T'ree Claws? Yah? He comes sometimes." Tank's eyebrows twisted.

"Three Claws is an old bear that got caught in a trap umpteen years ago," Hallie said. "Tank feeds him when grub is short."

Still Cap chewed ice.

Impatiently Tank asked, "You vant that ay count owls? Porkies? Skunks that wisit Loverly? Mister still comes around."

Cap shrugged.

Cautiously Tank peered at Cap. Then he said, "Suka, suka, suka?"

The sleepy look left Cap's eyes. "Have you been visited by fur-people you've never met before?"

"Ay tank this fur-fellow has been here before. Ay find footprints sometimes in vinter. This is the first time ay hear him in hot veather. Last night he come down off the peak, ay tank, and vent down-crick." Worriedly Tank added, "He bother you?"

"No, not really," Cap answered. "Made the hair on my neck stand on end, though. Everybody's on the move, packing up to go home. We thought we'd better check up on you. Want to go to Kellogg or Wallace till things quiet down?"

"Ain't nothing to get riled up about," Tank said calmly. "As long as you're around to do my toting for me, ay tank Loverly 'n' me vill go on like alvays."

"Good," Cap said. "I thought that's what you'd say." He included all the others in a sweeping glance. "How about it, gang? Are we staying, too?"

"That's what we came for," Trixie said sturdily. "All in favor?"

"Aye," they all said—including Miss Trask.

A small sigh was heard. "I lied," Di confessed. "I don't want to go home and scare all our folks to death. But I don't want to stay here and scare myself to death, either!"

"Don't fret," Miss Trask said kindly. "You know that Knut and Cap will look out for us."

It Had Hands • 6

MISS TRASK ROSE from her thronelike chair. "I do think it is time we hike down that mountain. It occurs to me that it may be a good idea to prepare our dinner before dark."

On the way home, Trixie wondered what else had occurred to Miss Trask. Walking close to Cap, Trixie watched the steady, rhythmic placing of his moccasined feet, the swinging of his shoulders, and the smooth coil of his tied-back brown hair. She tried, but she just didn't know Cap well enough to read his face. Had *he* put aside the worry about the sasquatch? If so, at least Cap knew what he was putting aside.

The group stopped at intervals to drink sparingly from canteens. About halfway home, during one of their rest stops, Knut snapped his fingers.

"Rats!" he said. "I forgot to pick up Tank's bag of dust."

"Sounds like a vacuum cleaner chore," Honey giggled.

Knut grinned. Smoothing back his bird wings of black hair in a gesture that reminded Trixie so much of her father, he said, "Maybe I'd better go back. I can catch up with you if you'll poke along."

"Oh, let's not *any* of us do *anything* alone," Di urged.

"I agree with Di," Miss Trask said firmly, and the others followed her down the trail.

"Okay, I'll just charge Tank's 't'ings' at the Mercantile," Knut said, matching strides with Trixie on the downhill hike.

A thin cry floated on the wind: *fleeoweep. . . .*

Di promptly threw both arms around Trixie's neck. "Where *is* it?" she squealed.

"Maybe I could tell if you'd stop choking me!"

"That cry came from a long way off," Cap decided.

When the group reached the clearing among

the tall pines on Champion Creek, it was apparent that no monster had visited their campground. Humans obviously had, though.

Trixie snatched up a piece of paper torn from a grocery sack. Large lipsticked letters read: BEWARE OF THE BEAST!

"Now, *this* is mysterious," Trixie gulped.

Honey pulled an envelope from under a water pail. "This one says, 'Go home now!' Oh, how awful!"

On the camp table's washable surface, somebody had written with charcoal from Cap's dead fire: EVERYBODY'S CLEARING OUT. ADVISE YOU DO THE SAME.

"I'm frightened," Di wailed.

"Look, the handwritings are all different," Trixie declared. "That means that several people have been in camp."

"That's right," said Cap, "and there's nothing mysterious, awful, or frightening about it. That guy from Walla Walla simply started a panic."

"Let 'em panic," Hallie drawled. "That leaves us with a big hunk of the Joe country for our private playground."

"W-We've already got too much space to suit me," Di quavered.

Miss Trask took charge. "We have work to

do. Di, suppose you peel potatoes. Mart will help you. Honey, we'll need a salad. Jim, fresh water."

Cap volunteered to build and tend the fire. Trixie, who hated kitchen duty, began gathering pinecones to use for kindling. A slight wind had brought down hundreds within easy scavenging distance.

As she carried them to Cap, who was splitting wood, a station wagon pulled up behind Cap's truck. A rangy man climbed out. Several children scrambled out of the jumble of boxes and bedrolls to cluster around the man like a litter of pups. The man watched as Cap formed a small mound of pinecones and dry twigs.

"It appears you ain't aimin' to take off," he said.

"Looks that way," Cap said pleasantly. He struck a match. Flames bit into the cones.

"Kind of wish there was some way to send my kids to Wallace for a while. I'd like a crack at that two-legged varmint. Whooey, think of that—Opie Swisher, first man in history to drop a real, live bigfoot!"

The heat in Trixie's cheeks was not from Cap's fire. Cap didn't look up.

"I couldn't get you young folks to take my kids for a few days, now, could I?"

The two Beldens were silent.

"Well, I reckon not." The man scowled. "Come on, kids; let's go. Maybe we'll be lucky enough to find friendlier folks somewhere along the road."

The ragtag group went back to the wagon and roared away.

Trixie let out her breath. "Jeepers, at least there's a person who's not panicking."

"He's doing just the opposite," Cap muttered. "All he's interested in is murder."

"Animals are *killed*, Cap. It's *people* who are murdered!"

"Well?" Cap prompted.

"Are you saying that the sasquatch is a—a person?"

"No," Cap said slowly, "but I'm not saying its ancestors didn't start out to be human."

In the early evening, while the group was enjoying the food they had cooked over an open fire, yet another visitor, a slovenly young man, appeared. He wandered into the camp and leaned against a pine tree. Warily Trixie studied the unkempt figure. Sunburned and unshaven, he had uncombed yellow hair and an untrimmed yellow mustache. On the other hand, he looked as though he could take care of himself in the mountains.

"Guess you've heard the news," he said, ambling forward. "There's a beast on the prowl."

"So we've heard," Jim answered for the group.

The man looked at the tidy camp. "Are you prepared to defend yourselves?"

"We have no weapons, if that's what you mean," Brian said, "but there should be safety in numbers."

"I wouldn't count on it," the young man advised. "Are you from around here?"

"New York State," Mart answered.

"Thought you sounded like outsiders. My name is Fred Swisher. I've got a camp downcrick a ways." He jerked a thumb in an indefinite direction, meanwhile staring at the plate of biscuits Miss Trask had just brought to the table.

Kindhearted Honey asked, "Are you hungry, Fred? We have enough to share."

"Thanks," Fred said, sitting down. "Please pass the butter."

Several biscuits later, Fred disappeared down the trail again, calling out a few final warnings about the sasquatch as he went.

"Now, there's another man with more on his mind than panic," said Trixie.

"Right—food!" Mart said appreciatively.

"Swisher!" Trixie suddenly exclaimed. "That

was the name of that other man—the one with the kids. I wonder if they're related."

"You'd think they would have mentioned it," said Honey. "Did they look alike?"

"Hard to tell, with all the hair on Fred," said Trixie as she reluctantly got up to help clear the table.

When the camp was clean enough to suit even Cap, the group gathered around the campfire once again.

"Want to tell ghost tales?" Hallie drawled.

"Oh, Hallie, you wouldn't!" Di wailed.

"Let's sing," Cap suggested, adding fuel till the flames leaped.

Trixie loved to sing, and so did the others. Just when the harmony was sweetest and she had the feeling that the pines themselves listened, she became aware of an approaching vehicle. Its lights swung in an arc, striking bark, brush, and boulders, and came to rest pointed straight at the rear of Cap's truck.

Three men crawled from the cab. A voice yelled, "Hey, there, Cap!"

Cap loped around the fire to join the men coming forward. "Hi, guys! Gosh, it's good to see you. Come meet my friends and relatives."

One voice said, "Look, we're due at Big Dick creek by midnight. Hurry it up, Will."

The driver pleaded, "I've got a story for Cap that he'll never believe."

In a jumble of talk and laughter, Cap drew the men to the fire and introduced them: Will, Jinx, and Bo, friends of Cap's from the Forestry lookout.

"Ma'am," Will told Miss Trask, "I don't want to scare you folks, but it's only fair to warn you."

Trixie heard Di's quick intake of breath and reached out to hold her hand.

Will drew out a bandana, mopped his brow, and burst out, "Cap, I just saw the doggonest sight I ever hope to see!"

"Spit it out," Cap urged.

"Like Bo said, we're heading south for Big Dick creek, coming from Wallace. Just before we got to the pass, I got this whiff of an uncleaned stable—where there are no stables. Then something stood up in the bushes. I swear it was seven or eight feet tall. It put a hand across its face to shield its eyes from the headlights; then it disappeared."

"It had to be an elk or a bear," Bo said.

"But, hands, Bo; it had hands!" Will insisted.

Cap asked alertly, "Anybody else see what you saw, Will?"

"I wasn't watching the road," said Jinx, "but

you better believe something happened. Will here was shaking like a leaf when he slammed on the brakes."

"You'd shake, too," Will argued, "seeing something unnatural like that."

"Just where did this take place?" Knut asked.

"It was at the head of that draw where the old log chute goes to the valley floor," Will said. "You know where I mean?"

Knut and Cap nodded.

Jinx turned to Miss Trask. "Don't worry, ma'am. That's on the north side of the saddle. It would take a while for Will's nightmare to walk this far."

"I'm sure it would," Miss Trask said. Trixie wondered how she managed to sound so calm. Her own heart was thumping like a bongo.

Cap rolled his jacket fringes around a finger. "I suppose you've had the word there's a sasquatch scare in the campgrounds here on Champion. Well, it's more than a scare." He told of his sighting.

Will stirred uneasily. "We sure didn't expect to run into bigfoot in the Joe forest, and certainly not here on Champion. I'd always considered him to be a dropout of the human race that stuck to the snow peaks of the Cascades. It doesn't make a bit of sense to find him this far inland." He squinted at Cap. "You pretty sure of your facts?"

"Yep," Cap said.

Will looked glum.

"I've been thinking," Cap went on. "I know they're checking the possibility of eruption of some ancient craters in the Cascades. I wonder if the wildlife is getting nervous and moving out. For example, on the main body of the St. Joe, near the town of St. Maries, there's an enormous colony of ospreys—eagles that moved in from the coast years ago when their feeding grounds began to disappear. Couldn't the same thing happen to the sasquatch?"

"Good thinking, son," said Will earnestly. "Now, I haven't been one to take the sasquatch seriously. Always thought it was an Indian myth, but lately things have been happening that are hard to explain. As I see it, the real danger here is human, not hominid. I don't want guns popping at everything that moves. And I don't want chiselers taking advantage of the honest fright of other people." He rose, hitched at his belt, and said, "We'd better be on our way. We'll look in on you in a couple of days. Now, use your heads, okay?"

"Yes, sir," Cap said.

When the truck had rumbled off down the

narrow road, Trixie stood up and said cheerfully, "Gleeps, that was good news!"

"What's so good about it?" Mart argued. "One more person has sighted a sasquatch."

"Yes, but this time it's so far away that we'll get a good night's sleep without anyone having to stand guard."

"Trixie's right!" Knut shouted. "Come on, let's douse this fire!"

"Let me do it for you," Jim offered. "You'll smoke your glasses." To the girls he said, "It's going to be pretty dark when water lands on these hot logs. You'd better run to your tents and turn on flashlights."

"Give us time to wash up," Hallie reminded him. Minutes later, she repeated her nightly invitation: "Wanna giggle and gab?"

That night, Di, Honey, and Trixie shouted, "Wanna!"

The Pack Rat • 7

LATER, getting settled in her sleeping bag, Trixie listened to the boys' shouting as they splashed icy water over warm bodies, down at the creek.

"This water is c-c-colder than Tank's ice-house!" Knut yelped.

"So's your brain, honorable cousin, if you didn't test the surface first!"

Trixie grinned. That was Mart, of course, and judging from the following series of sounds, he had a pail of water dumped over his head.

From her side of the tent, Honey said softly, "Doesn't it feel good not to be scared for a change?"

"Sure does, but— Oh, woe, it's all so strange. We're *living* with a mystery that some of the best scientific minds in the country haven't been able to explain!"

"The world, not the country," Honey corrected her. "Knut told me that Russia has a multi-million-dollar project under way to investigate the yeti."

"I—" Trixie paused, not knowing how to express herself.

"I think I know what you mean," Honey guessed. "I'm on the side of the sasquatch, too." Hastily she added, "As long as it doesn't demand an arm or a leg!"

"I kind of hope it comes back," said Trixie. "So you can see it for yourself, Honey, the way I did."

Honey stayed silent.

Long after Honey slept and the boys' tents beyond the cooking area were quiet, Trixie lay awake. Mystery had intrigued her from the beginning of her conscious memory. Here was her chance to learn more about a more ancient mystery than any she had ever unraveled. . . .

Just on the verge of sleep, Trixie heard a whisper of sound.

Quickly she turned her face on her pillow. Had Honey stirred in her bedroll? No.

Trixie raised herself up on one elbow and stared into the dark. At first she could see nothing, but then patterns of starlight and moonglow became visible. She could see the darker bulk of food chests and trees, and the pale expanses of canvas tents.

There—something moved. Something upright. Something tall. The dark body merged with the other dark shapes of the food chests. *Cre-e-eak.* That was a hinge complaining. A food chest was being opened!

Her heart throbbing, Trixie reached under her pillow for her flashlight. She pointed the torch toward the food chests, but she didn't turn it on. She forced herself to stay calm.

The only animal I know of in the woods that could stand tall and still open a food chest is a bear! she thought. *But would a bear move so stealthily? Wouldn't he bat things around until he tore open the chest with brute force?* Until she was sure that it was not a bear, Trixie wasn't eager to attract attention.

She sniffed. She couldn't detect any scent that reminded her of bear. On the other hand, she couldn't smell rotten fish or field mice, either. If that *was* the sasquatch, would her flashlight frighten it away, or would it attract it, as it would a moth? Once again, Trixie hesitated to find out for sure. For just a moment, she let her tense muscles relax.

The next thing Trixie knew, Honey was saying, "Don't stab! I surrender!"

Trixie bolted upright and stared around the brightly lit tent. Honey was sitting on the edge of her sleeping bag, lacing her boots.

"Surrender to what?" Trixie gasped.

"You, silly," Honey teased. "You're clutching that flashlight like a bayonet!"

"How *could* I have fallen asleep?" Trixie scrambled out of bed and out of the tent. Her bare feet touched pine needles and pebbles, but that didn't stop her from hobbling straight to the food chest she had seen from her tent. Miss Trask and Hallie were already preparing breakfast, but Trixie had to open that chest before she could even say good morning.

"Yipes, it's empty," Trixie declared. "So I *wasn't* dreaming!"

"You're not dreaming, but you are kidding," Hallie drawled. She walked toward Trixie, waving as if to test Trixie's vision. Then she reached the chest and looked down into it. "You aren't kidding!"

"What's supposed to be in there?" Trixie asked.

"A ham, bacon, eggs." Hallie raised her voice. "Miss Trask, our larder has been raided!"

Crisply efficient, even at this early morning hour, Miss Trask joined the girls. "My word," she said. "Perhaps one of the boys has pulled a prank. Mart, perhaps?"

"Oh, I saw what happened," Trixie groaned, "but then I had to go and fall asleep before I could see *who*. Oh, Miss Trask, please don't walk around till we see what kind of tracks were left. What we need is an experienced tracker."

A tousled head appeared through a tent opening. "Be right with you," called Cap.

Trixie hopped back to her tent and dressed as fast as she could. Even so, Cap was already talking to Miss Trask and the others when Trixie hurried back to the kitchen area.

Briefly Trixie told what she had seen in the night. As she talked, her mind raced—raising some questions, answering them, asking more. Suddenly she burst out, "It doesn't make sense that an animal would have taken egg cartons! Wouldn't it have bumbled around, making a mess, trying to pick up a pawful of eggs?"

"The wrappings are gone, too," Honey added alertly. "I should think an animal would have been attracted by the meat odor and would have torn off the wrappings."

The partners of the Belden-Wheeler Detective

Agency traded a glance. *Aha!* their eyes said. *Now, here's a mystery that isn't two million years old—let's go!*

Mart saw the glance, but before he could tease, Trixie snapped, "Don't tell us, Mart Belden, that you're not just as upset about missing food as we are!"

"Possibly more," Mart admitted.

Breakfast-making was held up until the whole campground had been examined. When Cap whistled through his teeth to call everyone back to the table, it was to report that no animal, not even a bear cub, had visited camp.

"Guess you don't count pack rats," Hallie drawled. "I heard one on our tent roof last night."

"Hallie, you didn't." Di wailed.

"Don't worry, Diana. If he steals your family jewels, he always leaves something in trade." Hallie marched off to the tent, calling back, "Let's just see what it is."

Minutes later Hallie returned. "I don't know what the rat stole, but he sure as shootin' left a prize." With tantalizing slowness, she spread long, thin fingers and exposed a small object in her palm.

"A rock," Mart said with disgust.

"Look closer," Hallie urged.

"A medium-sized, unexciting, downright boring rock," Mart declared.

Knut took the stone and held it to the light, turning it several times. "I hope the rat visits me tonight!" he exclaimed. "A few nuggets always come in handy."

"Nuggets?" Trixie squealed. "You mean gold?"

"That's the best kind," said Knut.

"Where do you suppose he found it?" Brian asked, from the area where he was making pancake batter.

"He sure as heck didn't snipe for it," Hallie drawled.

"There you go, talking over my head again," complained Di.

"A sniper is a prospector who doesn't bother to stake a claim," said Knut.

"I thought a sniper sat in a tree and took potshots at people," Brian said.

"That's not what it means in mining country," Knut said. "Crevice mining is a specialized type of placer mining. You see, one of the best places to find gold is in the crevices of the bedrock. Ever since the glaciers melted, gold has been collecting in those cracks. You even find gold in roots of trees reached by fast water during spring runoff. Another good place to look is in a dry creek bed."

"Maybe that's where the pack rat found it," Di said.

"Pack rats are smart, but not that smart," Cap said. "They're just curious. They're attracted by shiny objects, but they can carry only one thing at a time. When they see something they like, they just put down object number one and trot on with object number two."

"How big's a pack rat?" asked Jim.

Cap measured air between his hands. "Oh, about eighteen inches, and half of that length is tail. They're just big rats."

Di made a face.

"Enough about rats," Brian ordered. "Who's ready for my pancakes?"

Mart and Cap scrambled for first helpings, and the others were quick to join them.

Trixie enjoyed the delicious pancake breakfast just as much as anyone, but the back of her mind continued to churn with questions about the thief in the night. No rat had stretched to raid a food chest, and no man had skittered across a tent roof.

Shortly after breakfast cleanup, the girls heard sharp words coming from the boys' area.

"Uh-oh, somebody's really getting it from Cap," Hallie said.

At that moment, Cap and Mart burst from

their tent, Cap in the lead. Mart was apologetic, but beginning to get a little angry.

"Mart! What—" Trixie called, embarrassed that the clown of the Belden clan was involved in a scene with his host.

"Ssh!" Hallie warned. "Stay on the sidelines, Trix."

Cap strode to the trash can and dumped in a sandwich and an apple. White-faced, he ordered, "Don't let that happen again, Mart."

"Cap, that was a perfectly good sandwich," Mart argued. "It could have been put in the food box!"

"But it was in our tent—where you know it didn't belong—and now it's in the garbage," Cap said.

"What's wrong with stashing away a snack? I always chew when I read!"

"Not in our tent!" Cap said flatly. "And if you don't know what's wrong, let me tell you. That bear cub we've heard bawling has a mother and a father and brothers and sisters and cousins. They all have noses and claws, and I'm not about to have a bear in our tent just because it smells your apple. And bears aren't the only animals in the forest! How'd you like to wake up with a skunk sticking its nose in your sleeping bag? A rat bite isn't much fun, either."

"Contrary to popular opinion, I'm not stupid—I do live on a farm, you know," Mart said defensively.

"That's not bear country!" With that, Cap turned his back on Mart and stormed out of camp.

Clues • 8

MART STARED after Cap worriedly. "Where do you think he's going?" he asked Hallie.

Hallie shrugged. "He'll be back by dinner, if not before. When Cap gets hot under the collar, he goes into the forest to cool himself down. He's got quite a temper, for a birdbrain."

"I noticed." Mart whistled. "I feel like an idiot—"

"Don't torture yourself," advised Hallie. "Cap takes his camping pretty seriously, but he'll have forgotten all about your spat by the time he gets back."

"Should he have gone off alone like that?"

Trixie asked. "Has he ever done it before?"

"Happens all the time," said Hallie. "Nobody, not even the sheriff, ever worries about Cap."

Knut, noticing that Mart still looked shaken, stepped forward to ask the whole group, "Have you ever picked huckleberries up on the saddle? It's like being on top of the world!" His voice promised adventure such as they had never experienced. "I'll make everyone a deal. You help me pick a pail or two of berries to take to Gloria's mother, and I'll let all of you horn in on my date Friday night. Okay?"

"That's quite a trade-off," laughed Jim.

"But it's a deal," Trixie said.

"Come on, Trix," said Hallie. "Let's break out the carton that has the pails. We want to get to the saddle before noon, or we'll fry to a crisp."

"Aren't we going to trail that thief?" recalled Trixie suddenly.

"Skip it till we get back," Hallie suggested. "That food is gone, but we've plenty more. Who knows? Maybe the thief will come back tonight to steal the rest and we can catch him red-handed."

"I guess there's not much we can do," Trixie had to agree. She followed Hallie to the area of the neatly stored supplies.

Hallie counted out pails and gave half the stack to Trixie. The girls were carrying the pails over to the truck, when they heard Di scream down by the creek, where underbrush created its own mystery even in broad daylight. Trixie and Hallie dumped their pails into the truck bed and ran.

"Whatever you're doing, Di," Hallie shouted, "just stop doing it till we get there!"

"What if she's falling in?" Trixie panted.

"She can just stop falling!" Hallie answered. Both girls stifled a giggle at the mental picture of Di hanging in midair above the creek, waiting for an audience before she could splash down. They burst through the bushes to find Di on her knees in a deer trail.

"Are you hurt, Di?" Trixie asked.

"Who knocked you down?" Hallie wanted to know.

"I found a clue!" Di crowed. She guarded a bit of earth as if it were a gold mine.

"An egg?" Hallie drawled. "What kind of clue to anything is that?" She tilted her chin to peer into branches over her head. "Probably fell out of a nest."

"It's a hen's egg," Di insisted.

Trixie stared down at the broken brown shell and the yellow yolk and sticky albumen oozing into the black earth. "You're absolutely right, Di. That was one of ours."

Just then, the girls heard Honey's voice coming from somewhere down the creek. "I found it!" she was shouting. "Come and see!"

Hallie slapped her brow. "How many detectives are there around here, anyway?"

"Gleeps, we need all the help we can get," said Trixie as she led the way through cheatgrass, thimbleberry, ocean spray bushes, skunk cabbage, pussywillows, and ground-hugging plants.

By the time the three girls reached Honey, they itched from contact with pollens, seeds, and dust.

Honey, too, guarded a patch of earth. "I found a print of a bare foot," she announced proudly.

"How big is it?" Trixie asked, almost afraid to hear the answer.

"Nowhere near eighteen inches," Honey said. "I can't figure it out—I'm sure the boys stayed near their tents last night when they took baths."

After years of swimming with their brothers, Trixie and Honey were familiar with the approximate shape and size of their footprints. This was a wider print than any of the boys would have left.

"Does it look like one of your brothers'

footprints?" Trixie asked Hallie.

"Cap barefooted?" Hallie hooted. "That bird-brain probably wears his moccasins to bed. As for Knut, his foot is skinnier than a ruler." Hallie looked again. "Nope, that print doesn't belong to us Beldens. We all have long big toes."

"And there's a long-toed Belden now," said Honey.

The voice of Knut was heard, calling the girls to hurry back to camp.

"He must be ready to leave," Hallie said. "Come on, let's get at those huckleberries."

Trixie didn't argue, although she halfway wanted to stay where she was. She had the oddest feeling that she and the other girls were being watched.

The four girls saved time by removing their boots and splashing back up the creek to camp. While they hopped and hobbled across the campground to the table where Miss Trask, Brian, Mart, and Jim were laughing about something, Trixie burst out, "Honey, that's how it was done—that thief waded the creek to get here! He must have had his boots stashed someplace. Now, I wonder why—"

"Come on, you guys," Knut urged, "or it'll be midnight before we get there."

"Gathering our sustenance one berry at a

time sounds strenuous enough," said Mart, "but executing it in nocturnal obscurity is completely unwarranted."

"Come on, then," urged Hallie.

Miss Trask fanned her warm face. "Count me out, please. Somebody should stay here. Then in case Cap comes back, he won't find a deserted camp."

"Good thinking," said Knut. "But you shouldn't stay alone."

"I'll stay with Miss Trask," Di offered. "We can get dinner started, so it'll be ready when you get back."

Trixie frowned slightly. Somehow she felt safer when Cap, the young mountain man, was in charge. She asked Hallie, "Will Cap be back pretty soon?"

Hallie grinned. "He sure will if these kids get a head start on dinner," she said, with a farewell wave to Miss Trask and Di.

By the time Hallie, Trixie, Jim, Brian, Mart, and Honey reached the truck by the side of the road, Knut had opened both doors of the cab and was walking around the truck.

"Something wrong?" Brian called.

"Not really. I can't figure out why the cab smells skunky, when out here in the open, there's no trace of skunk odor."

"Thanks for warning us," said Hallie. "We'll ride in the rear." She was quickly followed by everybody except Trixie, who hesitated when she saw her cousin adjust his thick glasses and slam the cab doors.

"I'll ride with Knut," she decided.

Knut looked pleased when she climbed up beside him. "Sorry about the odor, Trix."

The distance to the pass was not long, but the higher they climbed, the warmer the temperature and the skunkier the odor in the truck cab grew.

"I can't stand it much longer!" exclaimed Trixie. "Knut, did you look for a skunk under the seat?"

"See for yourself," Knut said. "I've got my hands full of steering wheel."

Trixie bent low and scrabbled under the seat. She pulled out a flashlight, a tire jack, and a crumpled bar of chocolate. "Oh, here's something else." She pulled out a soiled woolen sock. "Yecch!" she waved it at Knut. "Here's our skunk."

Knut glanced, then looked puzzled. "I can't imagine where that came from. Throw it out." He added hastily, "No, that's littering. We'll have to wait and put it in the trash can when we get to the summit."

Trixie dropped the sock to the floor. A bit of green slime clung to her fingers. "Ugh—that's what smells. What is it?" She held her hand within Knut's line of vision.

"A crushed leaf," he said. "Probably skunk cabbage."

Gingerly Trixie wiped her fingers on the sock. Then she held her hand out the window the rest of the way to the summit. Her mental computer was clicking, and she scarcely saw the steep, climbing road or the great expanse of berry-covered mountain. Suddenly she burst out, "Knut, there's skunk cabbage all along Champion Creek!"

"It grows in boggy soil," Knut agreed. "What are you getting at?"

"The broken egg was near the creek, and so was the bare footprint," Trixie said, putting two and two together and hoping to get four. "Could that thief have been in our truck?"

"It's possible, but I can't imagine why he'd leave his sock."

"Wouldn't you if it smelled like a skunk?" Trixie countered.

"Guess you're right." He shouted through his window, "Hey, everybody, prepare to land! We have arrived!" Knut wheeled into the large flat space on the pass where several cars, pickups, vans, and motorcycles were already scattered about.

"I feel as if we've reached civilization," commented Mart as the group jumped from the truck, adjusted hats, and picked up berry pails.

"Why, Mart," said Trixie sweetly, "the rest of us are plenty civilized—what's with you?"

Before Mart could retort, Knut spotted a plant near the truck's front wheels. He broke off a branch and held it out for the New Yorkers to look at. "This is what we're hunting—huckleberries. Sometimes the plants are about a foot high; sometimes they're waist-high."

"Your waist or mine?" Honey wondered, indicating Knut's long legs.

"Mine," he admitted.

"Just so long as it's not Trixie's!" Mart added, with a wicked grin at his sister.

"Choose a partner, and don't get separated," Knut said hastily. "I'll take you to a patch; then we'll scatter out. Yell every few minutes, so we don't lose voice contact with each other. There are lots of ravines, and it's real easy to wander around and find yourself on a different mountain. Are you all sure you'll recognize the berries? They're small, sweet, and shiny, and they range from blue to black in color."

"They look like blueberries," Mart observed,

"but then, all berries look alike to me."

"You'll find blueberries here, too, and whortleberries," Knut assured him. "They all make good pie. Now, let's pick!"

Knut led the little band along the saddle road, then took a deer trail. It plunged downhill so steeply that his head disappeared before Trixie, at the end of the line, was sure which way he had gone.

"Gleeps," Trixie muttered, "why do I have this feeling that *I'm* the one who's going to end up on another mountain?"

A Very Special Kind of Bear • 9

KNUT REAPPEARED shortly, but soon Trixie saw Jim's red head disappear among prosperous-looking bushes.

"Honey and I are going on to that fallen log," she called.

"Okay, keep yelling," Jim said, already absorbed in his task.

Although Trixie was used to working in Crabapple Farm's raspberry patch, she didn't especially care for the tedious task of picking food bite by bite. Thinking about the past days' adventures made the job seem more pleasant.

On the other hand, Honey was used to being

waited on by servants but didn't mind getting her hands dirty. She quickly chose a clump of bushes and set to work.

Trixie moved past her and began to roll the juicy huckleberries into her palm and then into her pail. The pail she carried was one that the Belden boys had made by poking holes in a half-gallon vegetable can and adding a wire bail. It seemed to take forever to cover the bottom of the can with berries.

While she picked, Trixie appreciated the mountain's timeless silence. Far, far below she could see a green valley and a meandering stream. Mountains stretched beyond that, till blue distance swallowed up the distinction between mountain and sky. This had to be close to the spot where Cap's friends, the foresters, had seen the sasquatch, Trixie thought. Up here, it was almost easy to accept the existence of that strange creature—practically easier than accepting the existence of other human beings.

Trixie crushed a berry between her fingers, and the faint odor of skunk cabbage disappeared. She thought briefly of the thief, but for the moment, nothing seemed to matter more than this berry, and this berry, and this one.

Knut shouted to his nearest neighbors, Mart and Hallie, who replied in unison. Then they hallooed to Jim. After Jim called back to them, he shouted to Honey and Trixie.

"Can you hear me?" Trixie called.

Jim answered, "Hear you." *You, you, you,* said the echo.

After a while, Trixie realized that her pail was almost full. If the others had worked this steadily, Miss Trask would have enough fruit to serve at several meals, even after Knut took his offering to his girl friend's mother.

The back of Trixie's neck and shoulders felt hot. She noticed that Honey had worked farther up the hill, and she ambled over to join her for a while.

Just then, she saw a patch of extra-large berries. With her eyes on their juiciness, Trixie stepped forward. In front of her was an obstruction of some kind, but in the litter of weeds, it looked solid enough to climb over.

Trixie lifted her berry pail high and clambered up—but not over!

With unbelievable speed, her feet shot out from under her. Landing with her pail lodged miraculously between her knees, she whooshed down what was apparently an abandoned log chute. Trees and bushes whizzed past her astonished eyes. *I've got to stop!* she thought, but when she reached out, she was punctured by slivers from dried pine needles. She couldn't hang on long enough even to slow her plunge down the mountain. Those pine needles felt hot enough to burn her, too. As she sped, she became part of a great nest of needles, all tangled with a family of field mice, a chipmunk, and the slapping branches of bushes.

Just when she feared she was surely going to the very floor of the valley itself, she saw that up ahead a huge pine had toppled over, dangling one limb into the log chute.

And on that toppled tree . . . was a huge, furry, gray beast!

With bleeding hands, Trixie made one last effort to save herself. She failed, but at least the collected needles and her berry pail whammed the limb before she herself did. Trixie stopped with such a sharp jerk that her neck snapped back and she bit the tip of her tongue. Tasting blood, Trixie shook her head, not daring to allow herself one second of blackout as long as that bear—or whatever it was—was around.

Trixie's pine needle hurricane startled the great gray beast from its nap. It let out a roar, then rose instantly to its feet, seeming to block out the entire sky.

From under a shelflike brow, great red eyes stared at the terrified girl. Yellow teeth shone wetly. Huge dangling hands moved when the grayish shoulders shrugged.

Then the beast leaped. Bushes crunched from its immense weight. With a quick clatter of teeth, it turned away—and disappeared into the underbrush.

Not daring to move yet, Trixie made a quick survey, decided she had broken no bones, and concluded that she had escaped the beast for the moment.

But what was she to do now? She dared not shout for help, lest the beast itself hear her fright and return.

She listened with the intensity of a mouse trapped under a cat's clawed paw. She heard a clucking, chattering sound and then a by-now-familiar *suka, suka, suka.*

"Oh, no!" Trixie moaned. Could there be *two* of the beasts, conferring about how best to trap this unusually soft, furless animal that was herself?

So near to hysteria that she knew she would burst into wild laughter or uncontrollable tears if she made a sound, Trixie pulled her bleeding tongue between her bruised lips and counted silently, *One, two, three, four, five! One, two, three, four, five!* over and over. When the rhythm had calmed the throbbing in her throat, the tight rubber band around her head stretched enough to allow her to think.

"What *was* that?" she muttered. She had assumed that it was a bear, for what else of that great size roamed this wilderness, and what else was capable of standing erect and walking on two feet? But why had she thought *hands* instead of *paws* when that beast had stood up? And *why* did the odor of rotten fish linger to mix with the sickening sweetness of crushed huckleberries and the turpentine of pine needles?

Flies, gnats, and yellow jackets buzzed annoyingly, attracted by the crushed berries and the damp, salty fear on her skin. Trixie forced herself to stand. Clinging to the dangling small branches of the pine tree's limb, she gazed up at the distance she'd come in a few heartbeats' time. Nothing looked familiar to her. There was only one safe way back to the others in her group, and that was up that slippery log chute!

Trixie took a cautious step and discovered that the soles of her boots would grip the chute if she stepped firmly enough.

Before she could go any farther, she just had to do something about those slivers. Using fingernails and teeth, Trixie picked out the three most painful pine slivers. Then she gritted her teeth and began the climb up the long, steep, hot route that she had come down at such breakneck speed.

With each three or four inching steps, she paused to watch for the beast. She had heard that a bear staked out a claim on a mountain. Whether bear or sasquatch, it might return to assert its ownership.

Trixie could only keep climbing. Although keenly aware of fatigue, she stubbornly duck-walked the edges of the chute. Occasionally she fell. Once she slid back downhill but managed to stop herself, even though her hands were rubbed raw. She didn't *dare* return to that toppled tree. That—that *thing* might have slept off its bellyful of huckleberries. It wouldn't respond so peaceably to a second tornado.

Finally—finally!—Trixie heard the faint sounds that let her know the others were hunting for her.

"I'm over here!" she screamed frantically. *Here, 'ere, 'ere!* said the echo.

A thrashing among the bushes made Trixie cower down in the chute, clinging with all her strength lest she slide again. Suddenly Knut appeared just a few feet away.

"Where in blazes have you been?" he hollered, his glasses crooked on his face. Leaves and twigs tangled the bird wings of his black hair.

His eyes, like Brian's, were great dark holes in his skull. "And what are you doing in that log chute?"

Trixie tried to reach out to her cousin but fell from sheer exhaustion. Only Knut's quick leap and snatch kept her from sliding again. Weakly, she clung to her cousin's neck. "Oh, Knut, if I g-go d-down there again, I'll just d-d-die!"

"Okay, okay," he said, gentle once again. "Let me help you."

Trixie felt her feet touch ground. She sat and put her head between her knees.

"Well," Knut said after a pause, "at least you came back up the way you went down. Uh, why *did* you slide down the log chute?"

"It w-wasn't intentional," Trixie assured him.

Knut grinned comfortingly. "You're not the first person to make like a log and go down a mountain. Come on, let's get to the first-aid kit and fix up those abrasions. How about a piggy-back ride to the truck?" he asked, turning around and stooping.

Trixie objected that she was too heavy, but Knut told her, "Carrying you in my arms would be even more awkward."

When Knut strode into the parking area with Trixie on his back, Honey, Hallie, Mart, Jim, and Brian let out a welcoming shout.

"Are you hurt?" Brian immediately wanted to know. "You look—"

"Awful," Trixie guessed. "Gleeps, Brian, I think I'm basically all right. It's just my hands that are killing me."

Honey held one hand, Jim the other, while Brian examined them.

"You won't perish of blood poisoning," he decided. "And just as soon as we reach camp, I'll clean these abrasions with hot water and get those splinters out."

Trixie agreed wholeheartedly. Sticky and sore, she wanted a *whole bath* more than anything else in the world. And she wanted to lie down, close her eyes, and run the film of her adventure through her brain to see if she could make sense of it. Maybe she had seen a bear . . . maybe just a very special kind of bear . . . maybe. . . .

Brian helped Trixie into the cab, everyone else climbed aboard, and Knut started up the truck. About two miles from camp, he went around a curve and slammed on screeching brakes. One hand went out to keep Trixie from going through the windshield. Then he leaped out of his seat.

Trixie gasped, then shook her head to clear her vision.

There was Miss Trask. And clutching her arm

was Di. Both were trudging up the middle of the hot, dusty road. Di was in tears, and Miss Trask looked more upset than Trixie had ever seen her.

"The sasquatch," Di was wailing. "It got Cap! It got Cap!"

One Sasquatch—or Two? • 10

MART SHEPHERDED Di into the rear of the truck, and Knut urged Miss Trask into the cab with Trixie and himself. The instant the cab door closed, he roared down the mountain at breakneck speed. White-faced under his huckleberry stains, Knut asked Miss Trask, "What happened? What happened to Cap?"

"We—" Miss Trask gulped and tried again. "Diana and I were tending the fire, when we saw Cap cross the campground. He waved, said he'd be right back, and went to the creek. We heard an uproar, and when we got to the creek, we saw Cap struggling with—with some kind of—well, creature. We—" Miss Trask faltered again.

"What happened to Cap?" Knut almost shouted at her.

"We don't know," Miss Trask said shakily. "I stumbled and fell right in front of Diana. And when I got up, Cap and that awful creature were gone. They'd simply vanished." Miss Trask took a deep breath. "That's when Di and I ran. We both had only one idea in mind—to find you as quickly as possible. We didn't know what else to do."

Knut didn't answer. He just drove faster. When he reached the camp, he slammed on the brakes and roared, "Cap! Cap, where are you?"

There was not even an echo, only the *crickety-scree* of grasshoppers in dry grass.

Everyone was right behind Knut when he reached the bank of the creek. They saw dried sprays of goatsbeard crushed in mud. Ferns had dropped broken fronds. Torn out by its roots, pipsissewa's creeping vines looked like green twine.

Knut splashed across the creek, climbed the bank, and looked at the ground again. "No bloodstains," he observed.

Trixie heard a gasp from Hallie. Trixie put her arms around her cousin.

Hallie's muscles quivered; then she pulled away. "No mushy stuff," she said. "I have to hunt for Cap."

"Look in the tents, everyone; then spread out and search!" Knut ordered.

"I'm going to take care of Trixie first," Brian said.

"Fine." Knut loped away to peer into Cap's tent.

"I'll be all right," Trixie objected. "Cap's the one in danger."

"An infection won't help Cap," Brian told her.

Brian opened the first-aid kit and asked Di to bring hot water from the deep can that always sat among the coals of the campfire. She blinked her violet eyes as if the words were confusing, but she obeyed.

Quietly and efficiently, Brian made sure that both Trixie's hands and his own were as clean as very hot water and soap could make them. He painted her injuries with iodine, then took his pocketknife and sterilized its tip in the flame.

Trixie squirmed from the very sight of the knife, but Brian's fingers were firm yet tender as he pulled the splinters from her flesh one by one. Again she washed her hands in painfully hot water. Again Brian applied iodine; then he bandaged both her hands.

Trixie waved her two white mitts. "How will I take a bath?" she demanded.

"Look on the bright side—you'll get out of kitchen work," Brian said as he hurried away to join the search for Cap.

"I'll help you take a bath, Trixie," Di offered.

A short while later, Trixie emerged from Di's tent, bathed and in fresh clothing. The girls found themselves alone in camp, since even Miss Trask had joined the search for Cap.

"They'll all be hungry," Di said. She checked the food steaming in the fire pit, and Trixie found that her bandages did not prevent her from setting the table.

One by one, the others returned to camp, silent and discouraged. Spirits were somewhat revived by the foil-wrapped potatoes and corn Di removed from the fire. Hamburgers baked in foil with onions were appreciated, too. Each person washed a bowlful of ripe huckleberries, sugared them, and enjoyed the fruit with cold milk. Knut poured the rest of the berries into a large pail and sank the securely covered pail in cold creek water.

Hallie washed dishes with furious speed. She had said scarcely a word during dinner. Suddenly she burst out, "I simply don't understand how Cap allowed himself to get into trouble. That birdbrain can hear a pine needle fall!"

Di wailed, "How can you call him a bird-brain when he may be—when that furry beast—"

"Don't say it, Di!" Hallie warned sharply. "Cap will be all right. And I can call him a birdbrain if I want to, because that's what he is, isn't he, Knut?"

Knut smiled through his worry. "To understand what Hallie's saying, Di, you have to understand that she uses that in two different ways. One way refers to the *size* of a bird's brain, which you have to admit isn't very big. There are times when Cap deserves that name, too.

"But the other birdbrain—well, I wish I was one! A baby bird has the courage to flop out of the nest. From that moment on, it pits its strength and wits against its environment. After one round trip of migration, it has a map of its world imprinted on its brain. It builds its nest; it defends and feeds a family. It knows its friends, and it studies the habits of its enemies in order to survive and live in peace. It's up at first light and folds its wings at dark. It adds grace and beauty to the world.

"Most of the time when Hallie calls Cap a birdbrain, that's what she means, isn't it, Hallie?"

Tears spilled from Hallie's berry-black eyes and rolled down the lovely flat planes of her cheeks. With a boyish gesture, she wiped her face with the backs of slim hands. "I couldn't talk a poem about it, but that's kind of what I mean. Cap belongs out in the woods. If you put him in a cage, he'd go crazy."

"Maybe not," Trixie said softly. "Maybe he'd sing."

"Or break his wings, trying to get out," Mart added.

"The sheriff should be notified immediately," Miss Trask said.

Knut nodded. "Hallie, you can hold the fort here, while I drive to Wallace. I can pick up a few supplies at the same time. Oh, and Tank's things, too." Knut snapped his fingers. "Miss Trask, which direction did Cap come from when he crossed the campground?"

"I see what you mean," she answered thoughtfully. "He came from the direction of Mr. Anderson's, so perhaps that's where he'd been."

"Then I'm not going to sit around twiddling my thumbs, waiting for morning," Hallie announced. "Knut, while you drive to Wallace,

I'll go to Tank's to see if he can tell us something about Cap."

"Not alone, either of you!" Miss Trask said.

"Di, would you like to go with me?" Knut invited.

Di agreed instantly, confessing, "That sounds much safer than climbing up to Tank's in the dark."

"I'll go with Hallie," Jim volunteered, and so did Honey and Mart. Brian decided to stay in camp, in case an injured Cap returned. Miss Trask pledged to keep a giant campfire blazing. Trixie wavered, unsure of whether she'd be more of a hindrance than a help, with her bandaged hands.

"I'll carry two flashlights if your hands hurt," Honey offered, and Trixie's mind was made up.

"Okay, kids, let's get crackin'!" Hallie ordered. "Extra flashlight batteries for everybody, and a first-aid kit for you, Jim."

Miss Trask hurriedly made out a list of supplies they needed at camp and handed it to Knut. Meanwhile, Knut filled a large plastic carton with huckleberries, explaining in a low voice to Hallie, "I'll stop at Gloria's before I come back. If we need to get in touch with Mom and Dad, she'll do it for us."

A little shakily, Hallie said, "They're photographing llamas on the hindside of nowhere. How can she call them?"

"Maybe she can call Dad's mine office and let them take it from there," Knut said.

Overhearing their conversation, Trixie was glad she had stay-at-home parents. "I'm glad my dad is a plain old banker in Sleepyside-on-the-Hudson and not a mining engineer traveling all over the world," she whispered to Honey.

"Poor Hallie," Honey murmured. "It must be ghastly to have one's brother simply disappear. I'd simply die if that happened to Jim."

"Don't take any chances," Knut advised as he and Di prepared to leave.

"And don't drive too fast," Hallie answered.

"Chin up, sis," Knut called. "Our birdbrain's going to be all right."

"But he needs help," Hallie muttered. "That's a switch, isn't it?"

"We all need help sometimes," Honey said, linking arms with Hallie while Knut and Di left camp in a spray of pine needles.

When canteens were filled and sweaters collected, Hallie told Miss Trask, "We have plenty of time to get to Tank's before total dark, and it's all downhill on the way home. We won't be late if. . . ."

If. Trixie marched with that word as she climbed the mountain to the ancient dry creek bed where Tank had his mine, his cabin, and his garden.

"Can you believe this is real?" Trixie asked Honey, her trail partner. "Until a few days ago, I'd never even heard of the Joe country."

"Or a sasquatch." Honey shivered.

When the little group reached the first resting place, there was no singing, no teasing, and no laughing. They simply took a drink of water and then continued to climb.

Trixie tried not to think of the beast on the saddle. If she concentrated on the size and weight of it, she knew she would dash headlong down the mountain, screaming at the top of her lungs. She would zip herself, head and all, into her sleeping bag and. . . .

Of all the idiots! Trixie scolded herself. *You* know *that beast is north of the saddle, Trixie Belden. Di is the one heading in that direction, not you.*

Suddenly Trixie screamed, "Stop!"

Instantly she was surrounded by Jim, Mart, Hallie, and Honey. "Are you hurt?" . . . "What did you see?" . . . "What did you hear?" The questions tumbled around Trixie's ears like corn in a popper.

"The sasquatch *couldn't* have carried Cap off, because the sasquatch is north of the saddle! It's right up there where Cap's friend said he saw him!"

"You know something that you're not telling us," Hallie accused.

In as few words as possible, Trixie told of her meeting with the beast. "It was so scary that I didn't want to talk about it," she finished.

"There've been several encounters this summer," said Hallie. "They've all been reported and investigated thoroughly, but no one's been hurt. Unless—"

"No 'unless,' " Trixie insisted. "Cap was miles from the sasquatch when he had that fight at the creek."

"Unless the sasquatch has a mate," Mart put in without thinking.

Hallie looked so crushed at this suggestion that Honey cried, "Don't even think of that, Mart. Hallie, has anybody ever suggested there might be two?"

"No," Hallie said dully.

Although the sun was down, dim light lingered in the clearing when the group reached Tank's garden.

Hallie looked worried. "Tank always takes down his flag and lights a lantern in his yard at sundown. There's the flag, and the light isn't lit." Tired as she was, Hallie began to run.

Behind her, the other Bob-Whites stared with dismay. The cabin door stood open. The yard was littered with Tank's belongings and food supplies.

A Noise and a Scream • 11

THE YOUNG PEOPLE made a thorough search of the grounds, but they found no sign of the old miner. They gathered his scattered food supplies and returned them to the cabin and the ice cave.

When they rested a moment, they saw Tank's magnificent chair among the remaining debris. The seat and back were torn, and two of the legs were broken completely off. With angry tears, Honey carefully collected the pieces and placed them just inside the cabin door.

While Hallie picked up the rest of the things and put them away, Trixie noticed something caught in the hasp of the door to the ice cave. Because of her bandages, she could only point. Jim pulled a tuft of fur from the metal hasp, rolled it between his fingers, then put it in his pocket.

Before Jim or Trixie could mention the strange clue, Hallie said, "I don't like this at all. I think we should hightail it back to camp before anything else weird happens around here."

"I second the motion," Honey said nervously.

On the way home, flashlight beams shifted with each downward step taken. Stumps, boulders, and even the trees themselves took on monstrous shapes. Lights reflected in the eyes of night feeders. In the open areas, bats swooped after insects. Boots clinked, scraped, or thudded. Instinctively, Trixie listened to be sure that no extra pair of feet added to the scuffling noises.

"I hope Knut and Di are back by the time we reach camp," Hallie said. "Wait till he hears about Tank."

"Poor Di," said Jim. "She stayed in camp because she felt safe with Miss Trask, and that's where the sasquatch showed up. Now she's crossing the saddle twice tonight, and there's a sasquatch there, too!"

Trixie was silent. She supposed there *could* be

two of the beasts, but she wasn't convinced yet that they were dangerous. They were scary, though, she was thinking as she reviewed what she herself knew about them: She had heard the creature's mournful cry in the night; she had seen its huge footprint; she had heard one story told by Cap's friend Will; she had seen its ghostly bulk in the first light of day, and had descended like a human tornado on its sleeping place at noon.

But in all these things, she had sensed no real menace. A displaced animal was trying to adjust to a new environment while not yet able to sort enemies from friends.

Certainly it was big enough to have caused trouble with the foresters in their pickup. *It could have attacked me*, Trixie thought, *but it didn't.* Why, then, had the monster fought with Cap and perhaps with Tank?

"What would make Cap mad enough to fight?" Trixie wondered aloud.

"He'd fight for somebody younger or smaller or weaker, at the drop of a hat," said Hallie.

"Or older?" Trixie suggested.

"He'd fight a whole army for Tank," Hallie declared.

"Would he fight the man who stole our food?"

"I doubt it," Hallie said. "I think he'd just

figure that the man must have needed it worse than we did. Cap would give him a juicy piece of his mind to gnaw on, but Cap wouldn't worry us to death by getting into a brawl and disappearing. Cap and Knut and I take care of each other. Those parents of ours in South America expect us to be stuck together with some kind of glue and at least recognizable when they get home.

" 'Course, the sasquatch hadn't moved in before they left the country. When something new is added, we have to make up some new rules. Oh, Trix, I don't know *what* set of rules Cap is playing by now!"

Trixie waved her taped and bandaged hands. "I don't know either, but somewhere there has to be some clue we've overlooked. There simply has to be!"

"I wish we had found that tuft of fur before Knut left for town," Jim said to Trixie. "I'd like to know what a lab test would show."

"What tuft of fur?" Hallie demanded.

"We found some fur tangled in Tank's door hasp—"

"And you kept your mouth shut?" Hallie broke in fiercely.

"Thou hath a temper like unto a Beatrix," Mart said lightly. "Try to see Jim's point. If he had told us he found fur in the door, we'd have seen bears and monsters behind every tree on the trail. Right, Jim?"

"Right," Jim said. "Look, I see the campfire!"

Brian was piling more logs on the fire when the five mountain climbers hurried into the firelight.

"I've made cocoa," Miss Trask called. "Brian, will you pass the cups? Come, Hallie, and tell us what you found out."

Hallie dropped heavily into a camp chair and rested elbows on the table. "A great big fat nothing—we didn't find Cap, and we didn't even see Tank."

Brian listened intently to the report on Tank's camp. "It sounds like somebody was hunting for something."

"It's a shame about that marvelous chair," said Miss Trask. "What could it have hidden?"

"Perhaps it was used as a weapon," Jim told her. "The moose that wore those flat antlers must have found them pretty handy for attack and defense."

Miss Trask shook her head. "That chair was heavy. It would take a great deal of strength to swing it."

"Maybe something heavy crashed into it." Jim pulled from his pocket the tuft of fur and placed it in strong light. "Here's a scrap of pelt-like skin that we found."

Trixie was puzzled. "If this is a piece of fur scraped from a living animal, wouldn't we see some dried blood?"

Brian fingered the fur and added, "It's a crazy idea, I suppose, but there seems to be more than one kind of fur here. See? There are some long, stiff hairs tangled in with shorter, softer fur. There's color variation, too."

Almost angrily Hallie burst out, "I wish that birdbrain Cap was here! He could tell us if this covered the foreleg of a gopher or the left hindleg of a raccoon."

Trixie watched in anguish as Hallie went off to sit by herself for a while.

Tired from the long day's activity and worry, Hallie was still able to perch quietly, her booted feet placed neatly side by side. Only her hands betrayed her inner turmoil. She plucked bits of wool from her sweater, rolled the scraps into tiny balls with long, nervous fingers, then stored the woolen balls in the palm of her left hand. Long lashes shadowed the high, flat bones of her cheeks.

Trixie moved around the circle to sit with Hallie. She was warmed by the smile of approval she got from Honey. Still, once there,

Trixie could think of nothing she could say to make Hallie's face brighten with her wide smile.

After a while, Hallie asked, "How are your hands?"

Trixie answered, "Fine."

Then both girls stared at the fire. Hallie returned to making lint balls.

"Listen," Trixie said. "I think I hear the truck."

All heads turned.

"It's not Knut," said Hallie. "It's coming upriver."

Trixie could hear the grinding roar of a motor in low gear. "Who else could it be? It's so late."

"Oh, 'most anybody," Hallie said listlessly. "Berry pickers who waited till sundown to leave a good patch. Strangers who looked at a map and thought they could make it to a motel for the night. Fishermen heading for home. Indians moving a summer camp. . . ."

The truck came closer, then passed the campground.

"I hear another truck," Honey said.

Hallie stood and dumped her handful of lint into the fire. "That's Knut!" she said.

Again Knut drove into camp instead of parking on the road. He helped a sleepy Di from the high seat of the cab, then began handing down the supplies he had bought.

"Easy," Knut warned. "There are eggs here someplace. And Gloria's mother sent cream for our berries."

"Ice cream, too," Di reminded him. "Packed in dry ice."

For the next few minutes, all hands were busy, storing supplies.

Then Hallie faced her tall brother and demanded, "Well, what happened? In the first place, who was in that truck that just passed?"

Knut looked surprised. "Didn't meet him," he said. "The only traffic between here and the pass was a sow bear with a couple of cubs."

"And a porcupine," Di added.

"Anyway," Knut went on, "I didn't try to call Mom and Dad. Instead, I asked Gloria's mother to call Dad's mine office for his location tomorrow. If they're far into the back country, it may take several days to locate them. Mom and Dad might take too many chances getting to a telephone or telegraph office and putting their own lives in danger, only to find that Cap had shown up in time for breakfast. We've handled big problems before and come through safely. We'll manage this time, too."

"Didn't you tell anybody?" Miss Trask asked

anxiously. "I mean, besides Gloria and her mother?"

"I went to the sheriff's office and caught Sheriff Sprute and a deputy on duty. I told them about Cap's disappearance, but everybody in the county knows Cap's reputation. The sheriff knows it's not unusual for Cap to go off alone for two or three days at a time. When I told him about the beast, he said he'll keep an eye out for him and he'll keep in touch with the Duncans."

"Who are the Duncans?" Trixie asked.

Without taking her eyes from Knut's face, Hallie answered, "Gloria and her family. The Duncans are family friends."

"How long does Cap usually go without food?" Brian asked.

"He could live off the land indefinitely if he had to," Knut said with quiet pride.

"I just hope he isn't hurt," Brian worried.

"We have to believe he's all right," Knut said soberly. "Ron Duncan—that's Gloria's brother—is going to come out and help us search for Cap." Knut frowned suddenly. "You look like a friendless group. What happened here while I was gone?"

"Tank's missing," Hallie said bluntly.

"Tank, too!" Knut polished his glasses and stared at the fire. After a long pause, he said,

"Well, the same thing can be said of both Cap and Tank. Tank spends his life coming and going without reporting to anybody."

"It looked like somebody had ransacked the cabin," Jim said and went on to describe what they'd found.

Knut rubbed his eyes, as much from worry as from road weariness. Then he managed a small smile. "Sorry about the mess we're making of your Idaho visit."

"Jeepers, don't worry about us!" exclaimed Trixie. "It's Cap—and Tank—"

"The best thing everyone can do for them now is head for bed," Knut said firmly, propping his feet up on a log. "I think I'll just sit here and unwind a little while until the fire dies down."

Jim moved a chair close to Knut's. "I'll sit with you."

Later, when Trixie and Honey were in their sleeping bags, Trixie could see two heads, the one black, the other red, bent close together. She could hear the rumble of young male voices. Her throat ached because there were no bursts of laughter.

Long after the murmuring in the various tents had ceased, discomfort in her hands kept Trixie awake. It was so quiet that she could hear the whispering, if not the individual words, between Jim and Knut.

Like an exclamation point at the end of one of Knut's sentences, Trixie heard a soft *fleep!* that jerked her head up from her pillow. The sound seemed to rise from behind her tent.

It was then that Di started to scream.

Pack-Rat Condominium • 12

HYSTERICALLY DI SHRIEKED, "Help, help; it's got me! *It's got me!*"

Trixie's bandaged hands prevented her from getting out of her sleeping bag immediately. She could see Jim and Knut spring toward Di's tent, and in another minute, the whole group had followed, barefoot, in pajamas, and carrying heavy flashlights. Miss Trask patted Di's shaking shoulders until she stopped screaming.

"For heaven's sake, Di, it was just a pack rat!" Hallie drawled. "I turned on my light the minute you started hollering. The poor little varmint was scared spitless. Between your screechin' and my light, he must have thought he was a goner."

"Are you going to be all right, Di?" Knut asked.

"I—I guess so," Di quavered. "You'd yell, too, Hallie, if something furry ran across your face!"

Knut lifted an object from her pillow. "See? At least your visitor left you a present."

That night the pack rat's gift was a safety pin.

"Here, Trix, you can use it on your bandages," Knut said.

Trixie caught it in a white mitt. "Ugh," she said. "It looks like a bug."

Honey picked up the pin and held it close to her flashlight. "Why would a safety pin be stuck through a little piece of fur?" she wondered.

"Let me see that!" Jim almost snatched the pin away and strode back to the folding camp table with it.

Everyone else followed, shoulders hunched in the night wind, while Jim lighted the swinging lantern. He took from his pocket the piece of fur he had removed from Tank's door hasp.

"Well, I'm no expert on furs, but these scraps sure look alike to me," he said finally.

Everyone had to agree.

"That pack rat didn't carry a safety pin all

the way here from Tank's cabin," Hallie declared firmly.

"Anything is possible, I suppose," Knut said, adjusting his glasses to peer at the fur again.

"But not likely!" Hallie snapped. "For heaven's sake, Knut, that little guy has short legs. He would have had to churn dust to make it from Tank's place to here since sundown."

"Maybe he started earlier," Honey suggested.

"He just comes out at night," Hallie pointed out. She snapped a long finger against her thumb. "You know what? I'll bet he has a mansion near here."

"A mansion?" Di repeated with a nervous giggle.

"Sure! He builds a great big place, two feet high, with a couple of rooms, so he has space for all his junk."

"Why do you think he lives near?" Mart asked, curious.

"Because he was drumming up a storm, even while trying to get out of my light. That's his alarm signal. Why would he signal for nothing?"

"Maybe he was afraid of the sasquatch," Trixie said, explaining about the one sharp *fleep!* she had heard. For the moment, she let that thought go and concentrated on the fur. "Animals don't use hasps, and they don't use safety pins. The connecting link between those two pieces of fur has to be a person. Therefore, isn't it very possible that—"

Honey finished her thought. "That there's also a connection between Tank and Cap—a man? One fur scrap was found at Tank's place, the other in Cap's camp."

Miss Trask threw the proverbial cold water on Trixie's theory. "But the beast *was* here," she said. "It struggled with Cap—Diana and I *saw* it. Anyway, there's nothing we can do tonight. We'd all better get some sleep."

Mumbling their good nights, the campers returned to their sleeping bags. This time, Knut and Jim covered the coals with ashes and dirt before they went to their tents.

Some time before morning, Trixie roused, aware of discomfort in her hands. She wiggled her fingers and fretted with her bandages.

"Are you okay, Trixie?" murmured Honey.

"Gleeps, I got my bandage stuck in my bag zipper. . . ."

"Let me help you." Honey crossed the narrow aisle, turned on her light, and freed Trixie from the metal zipper. As she started to return to her own bed, Honey tilted her blond head to listen. "Wh-What was that?"

"Check the food lockers!" Trixie urged.

Honey played her flashlight over the whole cooking area. "Nothing over there."

"We're just jumpy," Trixie comforted.

"You're probably right." Honey went back to bed.

But then the sound came again—the *suka, suka, suka* they'd come to associate only with the sasquatch.

Both girls held their noses and gasped, "Whew!" at the odor pervading their tent.

"Isn't that smell different?" Trixie whispered.

"Smells like plain old skunk." Honey choked, still holding her nose.

"If we weren't in the middle of the Joe country, I'd think some meanie was trying to scare us," Trixie muttered. "But—"

Honey sighed. "But who would do it, and why? Oh, Trix, it must have been a skunk. Let's try to get some sleep."

Just as she drifted back to sleep, Trixie thought of the vehicle that had labored upriver. If Knut had not met it, it had to be some place between this camp and the pass. *There's only one road* was her last waking thought.

Wednesday had been such a long, strenuous, and worrisome day that it was past midmorning when the young people awoke on Thursday. Then, like puppets whose strings are pulled by one person's hands, they all popped out of sleeping bags and into the campground at the same time. They found Miss Trask sitting alone by the camp table.

"Good morning," she called. "I have a pot of hot oatmeal waiting for you." Briskly Miss Trask began to fill cereal bowls.

After breakfast, Brian removed Trixie's bandages, allowing her to wash and dress for the day before replacing them. Hallie arose from the table, scooped up Trixie's dishes along with her own, and headed for the dishpan.

"Everybody else dunks his or her own," she declared. "I'm giving Cap till noon to come marchin' home. That gives me a couple of hours to snoop around here and uncover that pack rat's mansion. Maybe we'll find another clue there."

"I'd like to help if I could," Knut said, "but I've got to scrub out the cab of that truck with tomato juice and lots of hot soapy water. It still smells like skunk."

"That's not the only thing that smells like skunk," Honey told them. "Our tent does, too—or at least it did. I think it's aired out now." She swallowed the last of her huckleberries before explaining about the early-morning disturbance they'd had.

"There's something rotten in Denmark," Hallie declared.

"Or skunky in northern Idaho," said Mart.

Knut shook his head and lifted the can of hot water from the coals. "I want to have the truck in decent condition before Ron Duncan comes. We may need to use it."

Knut, Mart, and Jim began scouring and scrubbing the truck.

Quickly and expertly, Hallie plaited her long, smooth black hair. She coiled the two braids around her head and settled her straw hat with a slap on its crown. "Who's going with me?"

Trixie and Honey stood up, but Di held back. "I don't know what to look for," she explained.

"Can't you recognize a pile of sticks when you see it?" Hallie drawled.

"Or where," Di went on stubbornly.

"Just look for a pile of driftwood that couldn't be driftwood because of where it is," Hallie ordered. As she tramped out of camp, she paused to add, "Especially around a fallen tree."

Still reluctant, Di went with the other girls. Hallie chose to search the area of woods behind the girls' tents. When they had moved farther and farther from camp with no success, she led the way back to the creek to search its north bank. "Pack rats don't like water, but they like to fool the rest of the world by building near water."

Dutifully Trixie hunted for a trash pile. She also watched for eighteen-inch footprints and any other unusual bruise on the tender surface of the earth.

When Honey finally located the pack rat's nest, Trixie realized that she had passed that heap of broken sticks many times since Monday. It wasn't far from the spot where Cap had disappeared. A path, no more than three inches wide, led to an entrance barely large enough for the tiny mammal to squeeze through.

Hallie got a firm grasp on one of the larger sticks near the bottom of the heap. She directed Di and Honey to do the same.

"Lift when I count three. One . . . two. . . ." Before Hallie got to three, a long watersnake slithered out.

"It's a rattler!" Di screamed.

"Diana Lynch!" Hallie yelled. "We're too high in the mountains to worry about rattlers! And even if it is a rattler, it's not chasing you!"

The snake slid into the brook and swam off downstream.

"I'm never going to drink that water again!" Diana shuddered.

"Good grief, we get our drinking water from

the spring that pours into the creek," Hallie told her. "Come on, Honey, help me."

Honey tried, but the combined strength of the two was not enough to raise the lid from the prosperous rat's sprawling mansion.

"I'll get the boys to help," Di offered, from the safety of higher ground.

"Okay, you do that, Di," Hallie said, grinning.

Trixie was glad to see her cousin smile, even though it was at Di's expense. There had not been much to smile about for many long hours.

Having finished scrubbing the truck, all four boys returned with Di. They stationed themselves north, south, east, and west of the big trash pile, chose the sturdiest basement-level branches, and heaved not only the roof but also the top story from a home of many rooms and halls.

Each nest was lined with dried grass and soft materials like cattail and milkweed fluff. In several compartments, the brownish gray pack rats had lain curled in sleep. Confused, twitching big pink ears, they scampered for other shelter.

Hallie paid no attention to them. With a stick, she prodded the rats' treasure trove. There were tabs from soft drink cans, several dimes, bright pebbles, and some nuts from bolts that must have shaken loose from cars on the road.

Trixie was fascinated. Awkwardly she managed to handle a digging stick. Suddenly she flipped a small object high into the air.

Jim caught it and whistled. "Somebody would like to get this back."

In his extended palm lay a small gold locket. When he opened it, Trixie saw the smiling faces of a young couple dressed in a "gay nineties" style.

"Knut!" Hallie gasped. "We know those people!"

Tank's Locket • 13

KNUT PEERED CLOSELY at the small faces. "Those are Tank's parents!" he exclaimed. "Tank kept that locket in his nugget bag!"

"Are you *sure?*" asked Trixie.

Hallie took the locket from Jim, snapped it shut, and revealed the monogram "A. A." engraved on the front of the gold heart. "Astrid Anderson," Hallie said. "That was Tank's mother's name."

"That rat certainly carried the locket a long way," marveled Di.

Hallie looked distraught. "I don't know where the varmint picked up that locket, but he sure as shootin' didn't traipse up a mountain, chew a hole in Tank's nugget bag, and skitter all the way down here to stash it away in his hidey-hole!"

"I agree," Trixie said. "And when we go up to Tank's next time, we'd better hunt for the nugget bag up there."

Hallie spun to face Trixie. Eyes flashing black fire, she yelled, "That's dumb, Trixie Belden, just plain dumb!"

"Wh-What's so dumb about it?"

"Climbing that mountain and hunting for the nugget bag—that's what's dumb! That bag has to be right around here someplace, or the rat couldn't have stolen the locket. The only way the bag could get here would be if Cap put it here. We've been looking in all the wrong places, and that's what's dumb!" Hallie's voice rose to a shout.

The Bob-Whites looked at each other uneasily. Doctor-to-be Brian recognized hysteria when he saw it. He put his arm around Hallie's shoulders and said, "Ssh, ssh, everything will be—"

Hallie shoved him away. "Don't you shush me, Brian Belden! It isn't *your* brother who's been beaten up by a sasquatch and carried away—maybe forever!"

"Please, Hallie," Knut began helplessly. His face was as white as Hallie's was red.

Honey reached for Hallie's hand and squeezed. "We're all scared and upset. We can't think until we calm down."

"I can think!" Hallie yelled. "I can think that Trixie can solve everybody else's problems, but she isn't doing a darned thing to find Cap!"

Shocked beyond words, Trixie waved her white mitts.

"I know your hands are bandaged! But your *head* isn't! As for you, Honey Wheeler, you haven't any excuse at all. You haven't any bandages on your head or hands!" Unexpectedly, Hallie burst into tears.

Knut held his sister close and crooned, "We'll find Cap. Or he'll find us—we're a team, remember? We stick together."

"N-Not this time," Hallie sobbed. "I'm just all unglued."

Knut continued to pat and croon while the Bob-Whites stood by, concerned. "I know you are, but don't blame Trixie and Honey. None of us knows how to deal with a beast."

"Forget about the beast. Just think about Cap!" Hallie cried.

Hallie's wrenching sobs made a deep impression on Trixie. "Hallie's right," she said gently.

"We've been letting the sasquatch make pudding of our thinking. Let's just change viewpoints and see what we're dealing with."

"We're dealing with Cap," Hallie groaned. "Maybe he's hurt. Maybe he's hungry. Maybe he's. . . ." Her voice ran down.

"Cap's alive," Knut insisted. "Even the police think it's too early to worry. Of course, they didn't see the beast, but they're sure Cap can take care of himself. And how is it going to help Cap if we give up in despair? Come on, now. No more tears, please?"

Brother and sister looked at each other. Then Hallie pulled away and dug into a jeans pocket. "Darn it, not even a tissue when I need it."

"Here, take mine," Honey offered, handing her a neatly folded, clean tissue.

Hallie blew her nose vigorously and swiped her eyes with the backs of both hands. Then she faced the Bob-Whites. "I'm sorry," she said, trying a small smile.

"Don't be," Brian advised. "You needed that, and in a way, so did we, Hallie. You cried for all of us. Now, let's get to work. I think a Bob-White meeting might be in order."

"Right here?" Di protested.

"There aren't any more snakes," said Trixie.

"How do *you* know?" Di asked.

"Well, *I* know!" Hallie said. "If there's a snake left within a mile, he's totally without sense!"

"Come on, Di, sit by me," Mart invited. "I promise to protect you from any and all reptilian animals that creep and crawl and grovel." Mart traced squirming motions in the air.

Di sat down beside him, but not before she had thoroughly cleared seat space with a boot toe.

When all were seated, Jim said, "Okay, let's consider the case of the locket found in the rats' nest."

"Pun, pun," Mart called. "We already know that the locket has a case."

"Knock it off, Mart," said Brian.

"Sorry," Mart said quickly. "What I really meant to say was, how do we know the locket wasn't stolen earlier and then somehow found its way into the pack rats' condominium?"

Knut stuck one long, bony finger into the air. "I can answer that," he said. "It's supposed to be a secret, but under the circumstances, Tank won't mind my letting it out. When we were getting ready to leave Tank's cabin Tuesday, he showed me the locket. He told me he wanted to give it to Hallie."

"Me?" Hallie gasped. "His mother's locket?"

"Tank's eyes are growing weak. He can't see his parents' faces clearly. He wants me to have their picture enlarged to fit a new bone frame he's carved. Then he was going to let Hallie have the locket. But I was listening so closely to his instructions Tuesday that I forgot to pick up the nugget bag, and he forgot to give it to me. I knew I should have gone back for it, when I remembered up there on the trail."

Hallie patted Knut's hand.

"Maybe nobody *stole* the locket," Trixie suggested. "Maybe Cap went up to Tank's yesterday and Tank gave it to him."

"It's possible," Knut agreed. "In fact, I'm sure that's where Cap was Wednesday. We have to consider that the trip to Tank's is three hours up and two hours down the mountain—approximately the length of time we used up with our berry-picking trip. Cap was seen in camp before Miss Trask and Di started up the road to meet us."

"What kind of mood was Cap in when you saw him?" Trixie asked Di.

"He smiled and waved," Di said.

"He didn't look like he was expecting trouble?" asked Knut.

"No, he said he'd be right back," Di said.

"What were you doing, Di?" Brian asked.

"I was checking the meat to see if it was done baking," Di said.

"If he smelled the food and said he'd be right back, Cap was no doubt hungry," Mart said. "That hike certainly puts *me* in a ravenous state. My point is that Cap might have been less than alert if he was washing his hands to get ready for a campfire banquet. The last thing on his mind would have been the possibility of an attack by a sasquatch."

"That's the last thing on anybody's mind," Trixie said.

"*Forget* the sasquatch!" Hallie said. "Say that Cap did go to Tank's, and Tank gave him the nugget bag and told him to hide it from me. Cap might have made up his mind in a hurry about a hiding place. He didn't know we had gone to the saddle. For all he knew, we were all over the place. He'd want to ditch that nugget bag where he could keep track of it and I wouldn't see it. Right?"

"Makes sense," Knut agreed.

Trixie stood up. "I move we adjourn the meeting, go back to the fire, and retrace Cap's route."

"Adjourned," Jim declared.

Back at the fire, the group found Miss Trask sitting in a camp chair, staring into space.

"Is there something wrong, Miss Trask?" Honey asked.

"I've been trying to reconstruct yesterday's scene in my mind. There must have been something I could have done to help Cap, but I can't imagine what."

Honey spoke for the group. "Maybe you can help now, Miss Trask. Can you show us exactly where Cap crossed the campground?"

"Certainly," Miss Trask said. She walked past the fire pit to the very edge of the campground. She turned to wave to the group, called, "I'll be right back," and walked on to the spot where the goatsbeard, pipsissewa, and ferns were broken and torn on the creek bank.

Up to that point, Miss Trask had moved briskly, sure of herself. Now she dropped her hands to her sides and said, "I don't know where he went from there."

"Did he do anything? Say anything?" Trixie prodded.

"He defended himself. The beast from the forest made noise—grunting and sounds of struggle—but no screams of pain or anger. I really don't know what it was trying to force Cap to do."

"Can you duplicate any of the action?" Jim asked.

Miss Trask thought hard, but shook her head.

"Once Cap raised his hand," Di recalled.

"Could he have thrown the nugget bag?" Knut asked alertly.

"I suppose so," Di said, her face brightening.

"Which way was he facing?" Trixie asked. "Toward the road or away from it?"

"Toward," Miss Trask told them.

"Come on, gang!" Trixie shouted.

The young people spread out in a fan, prepared to look into, over, under, and around every obstruction.

Trixie waved her white mitts and fumed, "Brian, how long do I have to wear this stuff?"

With skillful, gentle fingers, Brian unwrapped Trixie's hands and checked each wound. "If you promise not to climb a pine tree, I'll just do some spot-taping," he told her.

Trixie wiggled her fingers, enjoying their freedom. "I promise, I promise."

After Brian had applied waterproof tape to the sorest spots, he ran with Trixie to catch up with the search that was going on.

"Have you found anything yet?" Trixie yelled.

"An ant hill!" Di squeaked.

"Diana, you goose, that isn't an ant hill," Hallie snorted. "Somebody's littering again."

"Don't look at me!" Mart said hastily. "I've had my lecture. I learn fast."

Trixie thought of the food thief. Cap's disappearance had pushed out of her mind Trixie's determination to search for the thief. "Is it another broken egg?" she called.

"Ugh! Come and see for yourself," Di said. "I simply don't understand why you and Hallie are interested in messy, squirmy, crawling things!"

Trixie raced over and prodded a scrap of food of some kind with a stick. She watched ants try to snip off morsels, even while their world shifted under their feet.

"Oh, it's just a cookie," Trixie said. Then she noticed its thickness and color. "It's a cookie!" she shouted. "One of Tank's cookies!"

The Stone-Thrower • 14

"THAT PROVES IT," said Knut. "Cap was at Tank's cabin. He must have brought Tank's nugget bag back with him."

"How big is a nugget bag?" Di asked.

Hallie measured an oblong of air, approximately the size of a slice of bread. "It's made of doeskin and tied with a thong."

"So little?" Di looked doubtful. "I thought—"

"I suppose you were hunting for a shopping bag," Hallie scoffed. "Do you have any idea how much that much gold would weigh?"

"An inordinate amount," said Mart, all set to launch into a technical discussion.

"Stop it, Mart," Hallie begged. "I search better when there's nothing on my mind. You know what I mean." To Trixie, she muttered, "So does Di."

"Ssh, Hallie," Trixie warned. "You should be glad Di's helping! After all, she did find the egg and the cookie."

Hallie's grin was almost normal. "And the pack rat likes her enough to give her nuggets and safety pins!"

Knowing that the nugget bag had to be nearby put new heart into the group's search of the campground. Still, they were able to turn up nothing more interesting than beer bottles and several cans.

When they reached the sturdy wooden bridge that spanned Champion Creek, Knut said, "I think I'll go on to the river. Remember that guy that ate up half our biscuits? He didn't seem to be in a hurry to clear out. Maybe he stayed and saw Cap."

"Or the sasquatch," Di fretted.

Hallie scowled but didn't scold. She simply shrugged. Trixie hid a smile. When Hallie had visited Crabapple Farm, she had been "best friends" with Di. Even here, in an Idaho forest, Hallie had chosen Di for a tentmate. *So what does that prove?* Trixie asked herself. *So far as I can see, it proves that Hallie adjusts to a mansion better than Di copes with a forest. But that doesn't change the fact that Hallie and Di really like each other. It's a good thing they do, because we've enough trouble as it is.*

"Come on, Di," Hallie said. "Let's mosey up the road and see what became of that invisible truck from last night."

"What does a truck have to do with anything?" Di grumbled.

"Maybe nothing," Hallie admitted. "It just bothers me to know that Knut didn't meet it, when there's only one road. The driver might have seen Cap."

"It must be close to lunchtime." Di tightened her belt to show how lank she felt.

"Just wait till we find the truck," Hallie promised. "Keep your eyes peeled, and you may be eating that peanut butter sandwich sooner than you think."

Trixie and Honey fell into step with Hallie and Di, while Mart, Brian, and Jim tramped in the other direction with Knut.

With every step they took, Hallie and Di kept up an edgy give-and-take that just missed being an argument. Neither Trixie nor Honey interfered with what they both recognized as merely nervous chatter.

About a mile from the Champion Creek bridge, Hallie suddenly lengthened her stride.

"I said I'd walk," Di complained. "I didn't agree to run."

"Look! I think we've found it!" Hallie said as she moved even faster up the road.

Trixie, too, saw the spot where the shoulder of the dirt road had been cut by spinning wheels.

The four girls pushed through a tangle of syringa, thimbleberry bushes, and blackberry canes to find an old station wagon parked well off the road. An average passerby would never have noticed it.

The girls walked around the station wagon and peered into its cluttered interior. Dirty pillows and blankets were tumbled in a heap, along with a pick, a shovel, and several smaller tools that included a gold pan.

"I think we've found a sniper," said Hallie. "Say, haven't we seen this crate someplace? It looks familiar."

"Gleeps!" Trixie said. "This wagon belongs to Opie Swisher. He's that man who stopped at our camp with all those kids—the one who wanted us to baby-sit while he sneaked off to kill a sasquatch."

"We should have taken him up on that deal," Hallie muttered darkly.

"Anyway, he's close enough to help us if we need him," Di said.

"What can he do?" Hallie scoffed.

"If he wanted to shoot a sasquatch, he must have a gun!" Di reasoned.

"Well, Hallie, you've found the 'truck' you were looking for," said Honey. "I think we'd better head back. Maybe Cap has found his way home."

Hallie started immediately back through the thimbleberry and syringa bushes to the road. But when Di got her hair caught in the underbrush, Hallie was the first one there to help her get it untangled. Trixie was surprised at how very patient and cheerful Hallie was as she worked on the snarl in Di's black hair.

"You should see the syringa in June," said Hallie. "It's Idaho's state flower. It's white and waxy and smells like orange blossoms. In fact, it's called mock orange."

"If these bushes make orange blossoms, remind me not to have them at my wedding," said Di.

While Hallie and Honey were freeing the last strands of Di's long hair, Trixie lingered behind for a closer look at the station wagon. She could still feel the stiff resistance Cap had put up against this man's wish to "murder" the beast.

Scowling, Trixie circled the wagon one more time.

It was just by chance that she noticed a snag of fur caught in a door. Trixie pulled out the scrap. Even without checking, she knew that it had to match the fur that had been snagged in Tank's cabin door and the scrap the pack rat had left on Di's pillow.

Had this fame-hungry man really caught the sasquatch—or had it caught him? Might he have injured the beast? Could that have been the reason the sasquatch attacked Cap?

Trixie sighed, deeply and soundlessly. She sensed danger in each shadow behind boulder or pine, in each flip of a squirrel's tail, and in each tilt of a hawk's silent wings. Hearing the friendly-yet-not-so-friendly chatter of Hallie and Di up ahead—and even though Honey was actually closer to them than she was to her—Trixie was glad she wasn't there alone.

Then Trixie glanced sideways and found that she was even less alone than she had thought.

A man stood statue-still against the trunk of a nearby giant white pine. His rifle was raised, ready to fire.

More than anything, Trixie wished she could simply disappear.

Without a doubt, this was Opie Swisher, the

man she had seen in camp Monday. He hadn't even changed his clothes.

And he didn't look friendly. Trixie decided against asking him any questions. Not knowing what else to do, she took a step backward toward the road. She stepped on a dry twig, which snapped like a gunshot. The man stared at her, but still he said nothing.

He's standing guard, Trixie thought. *But he isn't worried about a bunch of girls. What else. . . .*

Trixie plunged forward to catch up with her friends. "Who-Who's hungry?" She greeted them with forced cheerfulness.

"What's wrong, Trixie?" Honey asked immediately, knowing something was wrong.

"I'll tell you later," Trixie answered in a low voice. "Let's get out into the open."

Silently the four girls hurried out to the road. When they reached it, they broke into a steady, energy-saving trot that would take them as quickly as possible down the mile-long stretch to the Champion Creek bridge, where they'd left the boys.

For some reason, Trixie's lips had automatically rounded into a circle, ready to push out air to sound the Bob-White whistle for help. When she became aware of what she was doing, Trixie took a deep breath. *Take it easy*, she told herself. *The tree squirrels are still working.*

They wouldn't be cutting down cones if they sensed danger. Cap says they're the biggest gossips in the forest.

Suddenly a rock hit the road. A single cone fell. There was sudden silence. Tree squirrels froze like statues. A gopher took warning and ducked into its hole in the road bank. Trixie wished she could shrink to its size and follow.

The first rock was followed by a second. This one barely missed Hallie's foot. Then one whizzed past Honey's shoulder. Almost at once, a fourth rock stung Trixie's leg before it hit the road.

Both frightened and angry, Trixie spun about, expecting to see the man who owned the station wagon, though why he should throw rocks instead of shoot, she didn't know. She began a sharp rebuke. It stuck in her throat.

Making no effort to hide, a huge fur-covered creature lumbered down the middle of the dirt road. Each time its two arms went up, another stone whizzed toward the girls.

"It's an—an encounter!" Hallie gasped.

"Do we run—or s-s-stay?" stammered Honey.

Di was speechless with fright.

Trixie bit her tongue. All the terror she had felt up on the mountain gathered in one great lump in her throat. Her slide down the log shute hadn't caused the beast to attack, yet here it came, hurling rocks without provocation.

Cap gave us the rules about facing a real, live, toothy bear, Trixie thought. *First, don't panic. You'll lose the race. Freeze. Face him. Back up slowly. Watch for a climbable tree. If possible, step behind a bush, then move slowly out of sight. When his ears stand up again, you're probably safe. But*, Trixie's brain screamed, *this isn't a bear. This is a sasquatch, and I'm not programmed for the unknown!*

"Let's run!" Di urged, white with terror.

"I—I don't think so," Hallie answered, just as frightened but familiar with the forest. "Running excites animals."

Surprisingly, the beast came no closer. Still, Trixie could see that it was not as huge and powerful-looking as the beast in the huckleberry patch. It didn't have the same great ledge of brow, nor did the sun shine on wet teeth.

"I th-think it's a y-young one," Trixie managed to say through clenched teeth.

After an uncertain shifting from one side of the road to the other, the beast stooped. It threw another stone, and with a gargled cry, stepped into the thimbleberry bushes that grew tall and thick beside the dirt road. A tree squirrel scolded.

Hallie wiped her brow with the backs of both

hands. "Well, that's that. The squirrel says, 'All clear.' "

"M-Maybe the sasquatch just ran out of rocks and is picking up some more," Honey whispered hoarsely.

"Well, while he's picking, I'm running!" Hallie declared. Pell-mell, she led the race to camp.

Not caring who heard or saw, the four ran for their lives.

Four Flat Tires • 15

AS IF ALL THEIR MUSCLES were controlled by one brain, the four girls thumped to a halt behind the truck back at camp, where Knut and Brian were struggling with a truck tire and a tire pump.

"What happened to you?" Hallie panted.

"Some creep let the air out of all four tires!" Knut answered, red-faced from both anger and exertion.

"We *need* that truck!" Di wailed. "We have to get out of here!"

"We can't go until the tires are filled," Knut snapped. "Use your head."

"Wait a second, Knut," said Brian. "Girls, you look like a sasquatch just tried to eat you for lunch! What happened?"

"How'd you guess?" Hallie drawled.

"What?" gasped Knut.

"It threw rocks at us," Trixie said simply.

"It chased us," Di shrieked. "It was trying to kill us—just like it did Cap!"

"Don't get carried away," said Hallie. "If it had meant to kill us, it would have used something bigger than a peashooter!"

Trixie spun around and grabbed Hallie's thin arm. "Say that again!"

"Say what?"

"It didn't have a peashooter, if that's what you're getting at," Honey said.

"But it had something," Trixie argued. "Or else why did it raise both arms to throw one little old stone?"

"How did it hold its arms?" Brian asked.

Trixie imitated the beast's action, raising both hands to eye level, the one behind the other.

"That looked like a slingshot to me!" exclaimed Honey.

"Jeepers, that's it!" Trixie shouted.

"What are we dealing with here?" Brian wondered. "Animals don't use tools and weapons."

"Except as an imitative action, usually taught," Knut added.

"This sounds far-fetched," said Trixie, "but could some human have caught and trained a young or disabled sasquatch?"

"Either that," said Knut, "or one of them could have picked up some of man's bad habits, just as a matter of survival."

Remembering the scrap of fur she had found, Trixie took it from her pocket and handed it to Brian. "Here's another to add to our collection." She related where she'd found it. "And remember that man who wanted to be the first man in history to shoot a sasquatch? Well, he's got a gun and he's standing guard. This fur makes it look as if he got his wish."

"Maybe we'd better go ask him a few questions," said Knut.

"After we eat," begged Brian. "My stomach is eating my stomach."

As the six walked toward the picnic table, Hallie asked, "Did you guys find anything?"

"Nothing. We didn't get to the river. We had the creepy impression that we were being followed, so we turned around and came back. Then we found the truck with four flats."

"Evidently somebody doesn't want us to go anywhere," Trixie said.

"Or is just plain malicious," said Brian.

"Where are Jim and Mart?" Honey asked worriedly.

"They're scouting around to see if they can pick up the trail of the sneak who let the air out," Knut said, scowling again.

By this time, they had reached the kitchen area, where they found foil-covered food on the camp table.

"I wasn't sure when you'd return," Miss Trask told them, "so I thought I'd have something ready for whenever you came."

Hallie tore the wrapping from a huge stack of sandwiches. "Bless Miss Trask," she said fervently. "Help yourselves, everybody. I'll whomp up some lemonade."

"It's already whomped up," Brian said, lifting a covered plastic pitcher. "Hold out your glasses. I'll pour."

"We'll call the society editor of the 'Sasquatch Gazette' and tell her you poured," Knut said. He tried to sound cheerful but failed.

There was a sound of movement. The whole group stopped chewing and waited to see what emerged from the brushy undergrowth.

Jim and Mart came out of the woods.

"What did you find?" asked Knut.

"Nothing," Mart said briefly.

"Not even a track," Jim added. "All of us have been tramping around so much that a dozen thieves could have come and gone, mixing their tracks with ours, and we wouldn't know the difference."

"Cap would," Hallie said loyally.

"Well, Cap's not here," Mart said flatly. "Although I'm sure he soon will be," he added hastily.

When appetites were satisfied, reports were given of everyone's findings so far. It seemed important to Trixie that each person know as much as every other member of the group. Lacking some small bit of information could put the whole group in more danger than they were already facing—and that was quite enough.

"Well, who's ready to go to the mine to check up on Tank?" Hallie asked. "We can get back before dark if we don't waste time."

Knut polished his thick glasses. "Hallie, I know you're worried about Tank, and so am I. But we both know he could have gone out tramping around someplace without locking his door. A bear could have gotten into the cabin and messed things up. It's happened before. For us, Cap must come first. I think we have to follow every possible clue while the trail is fresh enough to follow. I'm going back over the ground to look for that nugget bag, and then I'm going to check that man with the gun."

"Cap *was* at Tank's—I found the cookie to prove it!" Diana reminded him.

"Cap wasn't attacked by the sasquatch for a bear-grease cookie," Knut said. "He should be home by this time. Cap's a loner, but he just wouldn't leave Hallie and me to worry if he could prevent it. If he could mark his trail, he would. That's why I keep thinking that nugget bag is a trail marker."

He turned on his heel and started across the campground on the trail to the creek. Like the tail on a kite, the rest of the young people, and Miss Trask, straggled along behind.

The Stone-Thrower Again • 16

THIS TIME, Knut assigned sections to everyone. Trixie and Honey were left at the scene of the fight between Cap and the monster. Black mud, skunk cabbage, watercress, wild carrots, and a host of unfamiliar plants were a mishmash of color and smells.

Trixie sat on her heels to study the swampy area. She flinched when a snake darted its tongue, sensing her location. It slid smoothly into a hole under a pine, taking its time. A blue-tailed lizard skittered, now here, now gone, as fast as the eye could wink. Noisy nuthatches moved in short jerks over trunks and branches of pines. A woodpecker jarred the air while it drilled for insect larvae. A mouse watched with bright-eyed caution, then disappeared into a patch of ripe grass.

Trixie absorbed the peace of time and place, even while she tried to sort out what belonged here and what did not. There were the usual beer cans, candy wrappers, soggy cigarettes, and paper matches. Over there was an exposed area of metal, smaller than a penknife. Trixie would have overlooked it but for the way the light slanted. She chose a dry twig and broke it to form a sharp point. Then she walked clear of existing bootprints to poke the stick into wet earth.

"Honey, I've found something!" Triumphantly Trixie exposed a pair of tweezers.

"That's a funny thing to find in the wilderness," Honey said.

"Yes, isn't it?" Trixie answered thoughtfully.

For an hour, the girls poked and prodded the mud and moss that edged the area. When they heard the others returning to camp, they sat on their heels to dip their hands into ice-cold water flowing over pebbles.

This time it was Honey who said, "I've found something, too." She lifted a bent iced-tea spoon from the running water.

"At least we've found conversation pieces," Trixie said. "Too bad I can't think of the right conversation."

On the way back to the kitchen area, Honey said, "A fisherman who ties his own flies might have lost the tweezers, but I can't figure out why anybody would pack iced-tea spoons for a picnic or a campout."

"A fancy camper, I guess," Trixie said.

"We found the nugget bag!" Mart yelled across the campground.

"And the stuff the pack rat traded for," Hallie said. "The bag's empty," she added.

"That figures," Trixie said. "Where was it?"

"Caught in the bushes, right where we found the cookie," Knut said. "I don't know how we overlooked it before."

"We were too excited about the cookie," Hallie said. She held out a hand to show what she had found in the pack rats' nest this time. "Di's barrette."

Di wrinkled her nose with distaste. "I'll never wear it again!"

"Suit yourself," Hallie said. "I'm real glad to find the button off my jacket. Buttons are hard to match." Into her pocket, with the barrette, went the button. "Now, all I need is thread and a needle."

"We found something, too," Trixie said. She held out the tweezers, while Honey showed the spoon. "Aren't these wacky?"

"What's so wacky about finding this stuff?" Hallie scoffed. "You're in gold country, and those are prospector's tools. There's been a sniper at work."

"The station wagon!" Trixie reminded Hallie.

"That's right—there were mining tools in that old wagon," said Hallie. "I wonder if these things can possibly have anything to do with Cap's disappearance."

"I'd say yes if it wasn't a sasquatch that attacked Cap," said Knut. "What need would it have for gold?"

"I don't know," Hallie flung back, "but the nugget bag is empty, isn't it? The pack rat ran across one nugget and the locket, but he didn't hoard Tank's gold. I poked around in every treasure room in that rat mansion. There wasn't an extra flake!"

Mart picked up the tweezers. "If that's a sniper's tool, you'll have to show me how to use it. I haven't a clue."

Knut sat on one heel. "Here's what sniping's like," he said. "You pick out a crack in the bedrock. It's all filled up with silt, sand, small gravel, grass roots, rotten leaves, bugs—stuff like that. You take your screwdriver, and you loosen all this goop. Then you scoop it up with a spoon and dump it in your gold pan. If you don't have a gold pan, a frying pan will work."

"There's a gold pan in the station wagon," Trixie put in.

Knut's dark eyes sharpened with interest. "Chances are the guy's been sniping long enough to have all the tools." He went on, "If you can't reach the bottom of the crack, you break open the rock with your pick. You put everything you find in the pan, even plants. Sometimes those little tiny hair roots are twisted around a flake of gold.

"When your pan is a little more than half full, you pour in water and shake the mess around and around. Gold is heavy, so it goes to the bottom. This is called panning. You keep putting in more water and draining off trash, till you have just black sand and minerals left. If you're lucky enough to have a nugget, you pick it out with tweezers.

"Usually you dry the stuff, blow out the sand, and use your magnet, till all you have left is gold dust. Then you take a stiff paper to scoop your gold into your jar—and there you are, ready to go sniping again."

While he talked, Knut moved his hands as if

he dug for gold. Trixie could see that Knut was truly his father's son, a mining man.

"Is that what Tank does?" she asked.

"No, not anymore," said Hallie. "He's a hard-rock miner."

Knut jerked a thumb toward the head of the canyon. "Tank found gold in an outcrop up there on the mountain. He staked his claim and has his own one-man operation. He doesn't snipe."

It was a silent and sober group that set about the evening chores. Knut stayed by the fire to make his own version of a hunter's stew. He simply opened cans of meat, vegetables, and gravy, heated the mixture in a huge pot, and served the food piping hot in cereal bowls.

Hallie toyed with her food.

"You're refusing to eat because you know what's really in it," Mart accused.

"I'm worried about Tank," she confessed.

"So am I," Knut agreed. "If Cap doesn't come in tonight, or if we don't find him tomorrow, we'll go check on Tank. I just hate to take out six or seven hours before Ron comes."

"Ron?" Trixie asked.

"Oh, Trixie," Hallie said impatiently, "we told you about Gloria's brother. He's coming to help look for Cap."

"Oh, yes, of course," Trixie said. She didn't want to say that she hadn't been concentrating because she sensed the presence of somebody or some*thing*, just out of sight in the stretching shadows of early evening.

Thunk.

A rock whizzed out of the forest, hit the plastic glass Mart held, and splashed his drink in a sticky circle. He demanded angrily, "What's going on? Come on, you guys, cut it out!"

"Count noses, fella," Knut said quietly. "We're all right here."

Honey had lifted a slice of bread to butter it. A pebble drilled a hole through its center. Honey dropped the bread and smothered a scream. Almost at once, a third pebble spanged against the jam jar and dropped to the tabletop.

Knut picked up the pebble and rolled it between his fingers. "This is river stone. See? It's water-washed and smooth."

"It's carrying around a supply," Jim said.

Nobody mentioned the name of the animal, but the one word was in each mind. *Sasquatch.*

"Shall we try to act normally?" asked Miss Trask.

Knut frowned. "Evidently it's stationed itself to bombard the camp. I think it could hit us if it wanted to. It must just be trying to scare us."

"Guess what!" Honey's smile wobbled. "It's succeeding!"

"To think that it's only got a slingshot," Jim said nervously. "It's really ridiculous when you stop and think about it."

"It doesn't feel too ridiculous when that slingshot is right on target," said Trixie, rubbing the sore calf of her leg.

A tear rolled down Di's cheek. "Isn't there some way we can protect ourselves?"

Trixie gulped. "W-We could build a big fire and make sure there's a firebrand for each of us to use."

Nobody disagreed. The whole group rose from the table, rushed to the woodpile, and searched for long sticks of wood to push into the coals.

"Now we should be able to fend off the beast until we can reach the truck," Jim said.

"The tires!" Trixie reminded him.

"We finished that job," Brian said.

"G-Good," Honey said shakily.

"Tell you what," Knut said. "I'll go bring the truck right in close to the fire."

"Oh, Knut, no!" Hallie cried. "The sasquatch will get you!"

"Not if Mart and I go with him," Jim said.

With no more discussion, the boys rushed to the truck.

When the rocks continued to fall on the group around the table, Trixie had a sudden realization: The creature had mostly chosen to bombard the five females.

Bear and Sasquatch • 17

BY THE TIME Knut had parked the truck right in the middle of the small camping area, the pebble-throwing had ceased. The sasquatch was nowhere to be seen, but stars became visible, one by one, as if hands snapped on electric switches. It was a beautiful night, one that belied the anguish of those gathered close together around the campfire.

"I'll leave the truck here," said Knut, "but I really don't think we should leave camp unless it's an absolute emergency."

"Have we enough firewood to last through the night?" Miss Trask asked.

"Plenty," Jim assured her.

No one was in the mood for a game or a song. Not even a common topic of conversation came to mind. Everyone sat on logs or in the camp chairs and stared at the fire, holding their firebrands tensely.

"I don't like this!" Hallie proclaimed loudly, stamping angrily at an invisible bug.

"What makes you think the rest of us do?" Trixie shot back.

"Ssh, Trix," Jim warned. "We're all a little edgy."

"I think I know something that might help," Di said shyly. "I could make fudge."

"I'll beat it for you," Mart volunteered at once.

"It'll never set before bedtime," Trixie declared. "It's not cold enough out."

"We could cool it in the creek," Honey said, catching some of Di's spirit. "That water's really cold."

Knut hesitated.

"Why would anyone display indecisiveness in allowing Di to indulge in her penchant for cacao cuisine anytime the propensity strikes her?" demanded Mart. "Without doubt, she's the most adept, adroit, and accomplished concocter of candied confections in our native realm of New

York. In fact, said fair maiden is probably the finest fudge fabricator in the entire geographical entity you refer to as Idaho, as well."

"I just don't want to attract company," Knut explained. "But, well, I'm not inhuman. I like fudge, too!"

Jim raked up a pile of glowing coals. Mart kept up an amusing patter all the time Di measured and stirred.

Trixie suspected that Di was covering up nervousness and fright in the only way she knew how, by making a treat she could share. Trixie wished she could think of something to calm her own nerves.

At last, Di declared the candy ready to take from the fire. Mart carried the pot to the table to cool in a pan of creek water. They kept track of the temperature of the candy. When it was cool enough for a palm to be put against the sooty bottom of the pan, Di beat the fudge, then added vanilla. She and Mart poured the fudge into a buttered biscuit pan and took it to the creek.

Di carried the flashlight. Trixie heard her warn Mart, "Don't set it where the water's deep—just on the very edge."

"We'll probably end up with frog-ala-fudge," warned Mart.

"Oh, Mart, do you really think so?" Di looked stricken. "I did put foil around it."

"I was just teasing, Di," Mart said contritely. "The foil will keep the frogs out—and insects and all the other little critters, too. Besides," he added with a mischievous grin, "I doubt that any of us will give them time to get at it."

The two returned to the fire. It seemed to Trixie that Di was in her happiest mood since they had heard the sasquatch scream Monday night.

Not much later, just as Mart had predicted, Hallie looked toward the creek and drawled, "If that fudge is cool enough to hang together, I'm ready to take it apart."

Liking center stage, Di skipped down the dim path to the creek.

"Need some help?" Mart called, following at a leisurely pace with his swinging flashlight.

"I've got it," Di called back. "Just hold the light on the path so I won't trip."

Trixie saw a pair of eyes glowing beside the creek.

Then Di shrieked, "Go 'way!"

Next Trixie heard a calflike bawl of pained annoyance, then a grunt and a rush as a second pair of eyes appeared.

Di began to scream—not a pack-rat-in-the-night

scream, but an open-throated shriek of terror.

"Noise! Light!" Knut roared as he jumped up and rushed toward Di.

All lights flashed on. Voices shrieked. Hallie pounded the water can. Trixie banged the dishpan. Brian whistled through his teeth. Jim and Honey snatched up firebrands.

"Throw that darned fudge!" Knut yelled when Di rushed into the ring of firelight, hanging on to the candy as if she guarded crown jewels.

A bear cub and its mother were in a whirling tangle, right at Di's heels!

Before Trixie could find a tree to climb, the bear sow swatted the cub and sent it squalling into the night. She hung her head and clattered her jaws, not at Di . . . but at the *sasquatch!*

That strange beast had suddenly materialized again. It swayed toward the fire, then toward the creek. It seemed as though it couldn't move its feet. Something flashed as it raised an arm to protect its face.

After an eternity, the bear's jaws stopped clattering. Her ears stood upright again. As a warning not to follow or get in her way, she swatted the air within inches of the sasquatch's face. Then she turned and followed her cub. In another minute, the sasquatch had vanished, too.

Trixie looked down at the dents she had made in the dishpan. "Sorry about your pan," she told Hallie. "I must have been thinking I was hitting the *bear* when I beat on it."

Hallie giggled nervously, then said, "I sure don't understand sasquatches."

"Me, neither," breathed Trixie. "Why would it sling rocks at people, then turn around and run from a bear?"

"I can certainly understand the running part!" exclaimed Di.

"You can?" Mart's round eyes were blue marbles in a pale face. "Di, you just kicked a bear cub!"

Di flushed.

"Whew, that was close," Knut said. "A mad mama can be a handful."

"You know, Knut, we did everything wrong," said Hallie.

"I know," Knut admitted, "but at least it was a black bear, not a grizzly. The common black bear is usually timid. That's the reason it's still common!"

He turned to Di. "I'm sorry I let you make that fudge. Bears are storing fat for winter hibernation now. In bear country, it's safe to assume that bears are where the food is."

Di looked down at the pan of glossy brown

candy that she still clutched. "So are Bob-Whites," she giggled weakly.

"Let's get at it before the bears come back," urged Mart.

Di went around the circle, doling out the treat into outstretched hands.

"I doubt that the bear will bother any of us tonight," Knut said, after listening for sounds that indicated the escape route taken by the bear sow. "Just in case, I'm going to stand guard and keep the fire going."

"I'll help," Brian told Knut.

There were happy mumbles as teeth bit into the candy that was set barely well enough to hold together.

"It didn't turn out right," Di apologized.

"Brian and I wouldn't know the difference," Mart announced. "We eat Trixie's fudge with a spoon."

"You eat it, just the same," snorted Trixie. "Gleeps, Hallie, you look practically cheerful. What gives?"

"It's the sasquatch," Hallie said. "As long as it's hanging around camp, it isn't hurting Cap, wherever he is! And there're nine of us. I don't think that 'squatch is going to tackle all of us at the same time."

"Not with this big fire going," Knut said.

"Ssh!" Hallie warned. "I hear a motor."

"It's Ron!"

Knut and Hallie ran toward the road, forgetting flashlights and ignoring the possible presence of sasquatch and bears, so anxious were they for news of their brother. Soon they came back with a tall, thin boy wearing a red helmet and pushing a motorcycle.

When hasty introductions had been made, Miss Trask asked, "Did you talk with the sheriff at all, Ron?"

"Yes," Ron answered. "He said he wasn't too worried about Cap yet." Ron turned to Knut. "Exactly how long has it been since anyone has seen him?"

"Fifty hours," Knut moaned. "Fifty hours with a beast! How could Cap have survived?"

"We'll wait till morning," Hallie said, "then we'll go find him."

Knut burst out savagely, "Wait! That's all I've been doing! Waiting for Ron to show up to help us search! Waiting for the sheriff to decide Cap's in trouble! Waiting for a chance to check up on Tank! Waiting for that guy up the road to shoot somebody! Waiting for the sasquatch to carry off another victim!"

"Knut," Miss Trask said gently, "I'm afraid we have no choice but to wait till morning. As long as that animal is nearby somewhere, we're only safe while we're here in a group by the fire."

"Of course you're right," Knut answered dully. "Stay together, keep the fire going, and wait for daylight. What else can we do?"

"Sheriff Sprute will be here by daylight if I don't go back and tell him Cap has shown up," Ron promised.

"It's going to be a long night," Honey sighed.

It *was* a long night. Not even Miss Trask was willing to stray the few yards from the fire to her tent. Nobody could think of anything to say worth saying, so they all just sat next to each other, brooding.

Finally Trixie could take it no longer. "The sasquatch in my imagination is a lot awfuller than the real one has been—so far, anyhow. I've got to do *something.* Maybe it's too early, but I'm going to make breakfast anyway. Who wants juice and who wants milk?" she asked.

"I used the last drop of powdered milk we had in the fudge," Di confessed. "I never even thought about needing it for breakfast."

"Well, we can improvise," Trixie muttered, circling the table to rummage in a food chest. "Where's the dehydrated orange juice? All I can find is peppermint drops and—"

"You're in the wrong hamper," Knut said. "That's Tank's stuff."

"And sewing supplies?" Trixie finished. She held up a large spool of thread and a long zipper. "Knut, are you sure you picked up the right order?"

"I gave Tank's own list to the clerk," said Knut. "She filled the order for me."

Miss Trask held out a hand. "May I see that, please?"

Trixie found the orange concentrate and mixed some for everyone, while Miss Trask examined the zipper.

"This is a heavy-duty zipper, such as one sets in a jacket," Miss Trask said. "What use would Mr. Anderson have for this?"

"Tank does his own mending," Hallie explained. "He makes things, too! When I was a little girl, he made a fur coat for my doll and a muff for me. Remember, Knut?"

Knut nodded but kept his eyes on the forest.

Fur. A light turned on in the dark corners of Trixie's mind. "Show Ron the fur scraps," she urged Jim. "Maybe he'll know what they are."

"Know anything about fur, Ron?" Jim asked him as he dug the pieces out of his pocket.

Hallie hooted. "Does he! Ron's hobby is taxidermy. He stuffs what Cap can't mend."

"Could this be sasquatch fur?" Jim asked, handing over the scraps.

"Sasquatch? Wow!" Ron breathed. "That's what all the scientists are waiting to see." Ron rolled the largest scrap between sensitive fingers, studied it for a minute in the firelight, then said, "I'm surprised you didn't sort these out, Knut. Don't you know what deerhide looks like? See? This is a little strip of deerhide that hasn't had the hair removed. And these coarse hairs come from a black bear. The only local animal with hair that other color is coyote. I don't know how they came to be all mixed up together, but that's what they are—deer, bear, and coyote." He blew on the fur and looked more closely. "And thread," he added.

"Thread? You mean they're sewn together?" Trixie asked.

"Yes, and it's a pro job," Ron said.

"The scrap with the thread is from Tank's hasp," Trixie observed.

"Then I'd say you have your answer to the order Knut picked up," said Ron. "Tank may have been making something, ran out of thread, and ordered more."

"Something big," Honey pointed out. "That zipper is extra long." Honey dangled the zipper in front of her own slim body, then against Jim, who was approximately the same height as Tank Anderson.

"I haven't had a zipper this long since I wore snowsuits and built snowmen," Jim said.

"Snowsuits?" Trixie asked, her thoughts racing wildly. "Tank was making a snowsuit?"

"It's a very practical thing to have in Joe country," Hallie chided. "After all, we have as much snow here as you do in Sleepyside, and it isn't shoved out of the way by snow removal equipment. . . ." Hallie's voice dwindled to a halt as she watched Trixie's face. She waited impatiently for Trixie to react to her sarcasm.

But Trixie hadn't heard a word Hallie had said. "The sasquatch!" she shouted. "He was wearing a snowsuit!"

"Trixie," Miss Trask said gently, "maybe you'd better rest a while and let me finish getting breakfast."

"Wait!" Trixie said, explaining hastily. "I didn't mean that the *sasquatch* was wearing a snowsuit, but that a *man* was! He was trying to make us *think* he was a sasquatch! When he ran from the bear, I saw something glitter. That must've been a flashlight."

Deer-Trail Shortcut • 18

ARE—ARE YOU SUGGESTING that Tank made that suit so he could dress up like a sasquatch and scare us?" Honey asked in utter disbelief.

Trixie shook her head vigorously. "No, someone else is trying to scare us—the same person who stole Tank's snowsuit, messed up his cabin, and made off with Cap and Tank."

"You could be right!" exclaimed Knut. "Except that's an awful lot for one person to do."

"And what's his motive?" asked Jim.

"Gold," Trixie guessed shrewdly. "Tank's gold."

Di's thoughts were still on the masquerading

sasquatch. "I just can't get over that that was a *man* who chased us down the road and threw rocks at us! I think that's mean!" She turned to stare at the inky dark. "And he's out there right now, waiting to plunk us with that slingshot."

"Thank goodness he has a slingshot and not a gun," Trixie began. Her words died. One of those fur scraps had been caught in the door of the old station wagon, where the sasquatch-hunter stood guard with a shotgun. She licked her lips and said, as if arguing with herself, "The fake sasquatch can't be Opie Swisher. He wouldn't have had time to get dressed up and chase us down the road."

"You mean Fred Swisher," Mart said.

"Opie Swisher," Trixie repeated. "The one who asked us to baby-sit his kids."

"Are we talking about the same guy?" Mart demanded. "Fred Swisher ate our biscuits, remember?"

"Two Swishers!" Trixie whispered. "Of course!"

"Are you suggesting," asked Brian, "that those two characters who came into camp Tuesday have caused all this trouble and may know where Cap is?"

"Exactly," Trixie agreed. "And Tank, too."

Jim's mouth tightened. "Then what are we waiting for?"

"We need a plan," Honey urged.

"First we block the road," Hallie said. "Let's turn the truck across it."

Knut agreed and added to the plan. "Near the bridge there's a tree that leans out across the road. Ron, you can chop that down while Jim puts the truck across the road at the foot of the hill. Brian, Mart, and I will close in on the station wagon. Trixie, you have to show us where the wagon is, and the rest of you will be stationed along the road as lookouts, in case the men run."

"I'm not sure I can do that," Di faltered.

"You kicked a bear, remember?" Mart reminded her.

"That was an accident," Di gulped, but she buttoned her heavy sweater to the throat and reached for her flashlight. She had a reputation to protect.

"We'll use the Bob-White signal," Honey said and gave a demonstration.

Miss Trask's station was the campfire itself. Everyone else hurried inside the truck. Trixie shivered when she saw that Miss Trask was laying out the first-aid supplies.

At the road, Ron, carrying the heavy camp ax, slid from the tailgate of the truck. He walked down the dim ribbon of dirt road to the bridge. Di was given the first station, after being assured that the bear was long gone. Honey blended in with the night as she chose the spot where the "sasquatch" had disappeared into the bushes after the chase down the road that morning. Hallie was left at the blackberry patch.

With her brothers and cousin, Trixie crept through the undergrowth that hid the old station wagon. Each click of sound, dislodged stone, snapped dry stick, or swish of living growth being parted by hands was almost more than she could stand. She could hear her own heart thumping like a drum.

Unexpectedly she stepped into a thick, yielding mass of soft fur. Her jaws clenched to keep from screaming. "S-Something's got me!" she gasped.

At once Brian's flashlight poured a puddle of light around Trixie's feet.

"The sasquatch!" Trixie choked.

"It's that snowsuit," Brian told her, breath exploding with relief. "We're on the right track."

Willing herself to stop shaking, Trixie whispered, "Oh—th-there's the wagon."

Knut, Mart, and Brian crept toward the wagon, prepared to jerk open doors and turn on lights before the Swishers realized they were surrounded. Trixie's thumb trembled on the switch of her own flashlight. After an eternity, lights blazed, and Knut shouted, "Come out of there with your hands. . . ." His voice died; then he yelled, "There's nobody here!"

"Yes, there is!" Trixie screamed. She swung her light and caught a glimpse of Opie Swisher plunging toward the road. Trixie dashed after him, whistling *bob*, *bob-white* again and again, to warn Hallie and the others that a Swisher was on the loose.

Trixie remembered the shotgun, but she realized she had to keep track of Opie. Brian and Knut caught up with and passed her, while Mart was left to search the grounds for Fred, the biscuit-eating sasquatch. Lights swung crazily, now that there was no need for secrecy.

"I've found the gun!" Mart shouted.

"Take it back to camp!" Knut shouted back.

Soon Trixie heard more whistles and knew that Opie had passed Hallie, then Honey.

As Trixie started toward Hallie, Hallie was heading back in Trixie's direction. "Where are you going?" Trixie cried. "We've got to hurry if we're going to catch up. Come on!"

"Not till I've put that wagon out of commission," Hallie said grimly. "They're going to have some motor trouble. You go on; I'll catch up in a couple of minutes." Hallie crashed through syringa bushes and on to the wagon's hideaway.

In no time at all, having completed her mission, Hallie was running at Trixie's side. Shortly, the two girls reached Honey and finally Di, who stood in the middle of the road like a patrolman directing traffic. "He's on the mine trail," she told them.

"Then that's where I'm going!" Hallie said.

"Me, too," said Trixie.

From the minute she had first made the connection between the sniper's tools in the creek and the gold pan in the station wagon, Trixie had been sure that gold was involved in Cap's disappearance. Now that Fred may have stolen Tank's snowsuit, it was possible that Fred might this minute be trying to find Tank's cache of gold from the mine. He would think himself safe. Tank had plenty of food, so Fred wouldn't have to steal from the food chest, as Opie must certainly have done. After the barrage of stones, Fred would think he had the mountain to himself. Well, he was in for a big surprise!

"Opie's trying to warn Fred," Trixie guessed.

"Then it's up to us to get there first," Hallie decided. "The boys are following Opie, but we'll take a deer trail that's a shortcut!"

"Oh, Hallie," Honey said doubtfully, "should we?"

Hallie scowled. "Those guys know what happened to my brother. If you think a deer trail is going to stop me, think again."

By this time, Ron had joined them. With no disagreement, the group started up the trail at a ground-eating pace.

The trail was narrow, but flashlights showed the hard-beaten earth. Trixie could hear the squeaking and groaning of pines, and the chittering, grunting, squealing, and swishing that was the night voice of the forest. Just when she had lulled herself into feeling safe, a deer flashed out of the dark, seemed to brake its speed in midair, and changed directions. Only a breath behind the deer, a big cat landed on the trail, laid back its ears, pulled up its lips in a surprised snarl, and disappeared.

"Wh-What—" Di gasped.

"Don't kick it, Diana," Hallie drawled. "That's a cougar, and he's no house pet."

"Chalk up a good deed for today," Ron said. "We just saved that deer's life."

During a rest stop, Trixie could hear the wild gargle of coyotes gossiping on the peaks. And once she thought she heard, *fleep*, *fleeoweep*. She shivered. With the revelation of the bogus sasquatch, she had ceased to worry about the real creature whose sighting had been reported in Joe country.

"I think it's getting light," Di said. "I can see a kind of band under the stars."

"We'll see first light from the peak," Hallie said wearily. "That's something to behold, isn't it, Ron?"

Ron mumbled agreement, then said unexpectedly, "If I had a couple of bodies to hide—"

"Bodies!" Trixie gasped.

"Live ones," Ron added hastily. "I think I know where I'd stash them away."

"They weren't in the cabin or the ice cave," Hallie cried. "We've already been there."

Trixie pictured Tank's setup on the mountain. A cabin, ice cave, pump house, and mine, plus a lean-to for Tank's wood supply, made up the list of shelters. "The mine?" she asked Ron.

"Oh, no, not the mine!" Hallie moaned. "It's so cold in there, and Tank has rheumatism."

"I wish I'd known Tank was missing, too," Ron said. "Sheriff Sprute would have sent the Search and Rescue Squad pronto. If he sent them out every time Cap and I hit the trail, that squad would be all search and no rescue."

As the group resumed its climbing, Trixie said, "Let's go over what we know so far. I think one of the Swishers was sniping on Champion Creek before we moved in and the sasquatch scare drove everybody else out. When we didn't leave, Opie tried to get us to take his kids. That would have kept us in camp, while he and Fred went right on doing as they pleased. Hallie, do you think they could have known about Tank and the gold he didn't take to the bank?"

"Sure," Hallie panted.

"Tank's a legend in gold country," Ron said. "He's been crowding his luck for years."

"If Fred was hanging around, he could have heard us talking about the nugget bag," said Di.

Trixie paused to catch her breath. "Or maybe Fred had been hanging around Tank's cabin and mine before we came. He had seen Tank working on the fur suit. When the panic started, Fred got the wild idea of scaring us out of our wits. He found out we were unarmed, then went straight to the mine, where he stole the nugget bag and the suit. He could have pinned the suit with the safety pin when he tried it on and found it had no zipper. He must have snagged it on the door hasp."

"When he almost got caught by Tank," Hallie put in.

"Well, if I was a thief and I knew a bag held

gold that didn't have to be picked up with tweezers, I'd help myself," Di declared.

The idea of a millionaire's daughter sneaking around to snatch nugget bags stuffed with gold almost made Trixie laugh, but not quite.

"That's what Fred thought," Trixie said. "But we kept getting in his way. Probably Opie and Fred took turns pestering us and hunting for Tank's gold. I'm sure—" Trixie paused, trying to think of any errors in her logic before she continued— "I'm certain that Fred was on the mountain when Cap visited Tank."

"Probably Fred jumped Tank the minute Cap left," said Hallie. "Judging from all the damage, it must have been some fight."

"But why would Fred have fought with Cap?" Di asked. "Does Cap know where Tank's cache is?"

"Nope," Ron said. "Nobody knows."

And if Cap didn't know, thought Trixie, *what would the Swishers do to him?*

Bob-White! • 19

TRYING TO PREVENT Hallie from thinking about Cap's fate, Trixie resumed her list of clues. "I think Fred must have tangled with Loverly or Mister some time Monday. Skunk spray is unbearable. He would have slathered himself with the first mud he found, and that was back there at the creek."

"Tomato juice is better," Hallie said. "I'm surprised he didn't steal ours."

Di stumbled, then recovered her balance. "I'll bet Opie Swisher wouldn't let him stay in the wagon."

"Even an Opie Swisher has to draw the line

somewhere," Trixie concurred. "He probably wouldn't even give him a blanket, so Fred slept in our truck. That's when he stole our food."

"I never did buy that idea of skunk cabbage causing all that stink," said Hallie.

Ideas whirled in Trixie's head as she forged up the path. "By this time, Fred had things going his way. He had us believing the sasquatch was after us. This gave him some extra time to hunt for Tank's gold. He even had the pack rat working for him!"

"The pack rat wouldn't have crossed the creek," Hallie reminded her. "It doesn't like water all that much. That means Fred must have hung around the camp when he wasn't up at Tank's mine."

"I know," Trixie agreed. "We're not far from the station wagon. I think Fred kept that suit behind our tents someplace and only put it on when he needed to scare us."

"We smelled skunk the night you got your bandage caught in the zipper," Honey recalled. "That must have been Fred in his suit."

"But why did he throw rocks at us?" Di asked plaintively.

"He knew we weren't armed, and he was still playing the sasquatch game," Trixie told her. "I can see that quite clearly, but I don't know what Opie was guarding with his shotgun."

"Fred, of course!" Hallie said. "Fred was back there in the bushes, getting ready for Halloween. We got the full bag of tricks a few minutes later, when he chased us down the road."

They scrambled along in silence for a while; then Ron sighed, "This trail is a man-killer."

"A lady-killer, too," Hallie retorted. She stopped so quickly that Trixie ran into her. "Ssh—there's the cabin! All the lights are on, and there's no sound."

Trixie found her way by the dim morning light to the window of Tank's bedroom. Empty. She was puzzled by a strange creaking sound, like tree limbs rubbing together in the wind. She crept on to the window over Tank's sink and found Hallie there ahead of her.

Hallie said, "Ssh!" and pointed.

Making sure her face was shielded by the deerhide Tank used for a window drape, Trixie looked. Minus his sasquatch masquerade, Fred Swisher knelt on the floor. He had already removed one wide, solidly pegged floorboard. He was working on another.

"Dumb," Hallie muttered. "Tank wouldn't hide gold in a place so hard to get at."

"How are we going to capture Fred?" Trixie whispered.

"There's just one door," Hallie said, with a strange look on her face. Without waiting for the group to form a plan of action, she rushed up to the door and jerked it open.

With a snarl of rage, Fred raised a long metal bar and stood up. "Out kind of early, ain't you?"

"No earlier than you," Hallie retorted coldly. "Where's Tank?"

"Tank who?"

"You know Tank who. The owner of this cabin. What did you do with him? *And where's Cap?*" Hallie completely lost her temper. She yelled and lunged toward Fred, prepared to throttle him with her bare hands.

With a little cry of fear for Hallie's safety, Trixie, Honey, and Di followed Hallie. Fred threw the lever. It missed Trixie and Honey, but grazed Di's boot tops.

"Go get your slingshot!" she yelled with unexpected spirit.

Fred's face twisted with anger. He reached for a floorboard.

From Tank's doorway, Ron warned, "Hold it, Fred. Stay right where you are." In one hand, Ron carried a coil of rope. In the other, he balanced Tank's ax.

"Get out of my way," Fred growled.

The girls backed up hastily. Diana stumbled against a footstool. Eyes on Fred, Trixie jerked Diana to her feet.

Trixie saw that Fred was advancing on Ron. With both hands, she picked up the footstool and threw it with all her strength. It hit Fred in the back of one knee. When it buckled from the unexpected blow, Fred stepped into the long narrow slot he had torn in Tank's floor.

In that split second when Fred's hands swung out to balance himself, Hallie snatched up a pail and clamped it over Fred's head. Honey jumped forward to help Hallie hold it on Fred's head. Di dived for the lever.

"We've got him, Ron!" Honey cried. "Tie him up."

"Here, Trixie, do the honors," Ron said. "I'll stand guard."

While Fred yelled threats that echoed inside the pail, Trixie tied the man's hands and ankles together.

"Just in time," Trixie said.

She heard Opie Swisher's nasal, tired shout: "Fred, run, son!" Soon he stumbled across the yard, croaking hoarsely, "Run, Fred!" After struggling so long up the mountain trail, Opie was exhausted. Ron stepped to the middle of the doorway at the same moment that Opie tried to enter. Opie simply raised his hands and gulped, "You got me. Now, how did you git ahead of me on that there trail?" He didn't even fight when Ron used a piece of the rope to tie him up.

No one answered him. The four girls left the cabin and stumbled toward the garden, knees trembling with relief and tiredness. Together they signaled, *Bob, bob-white! Bob, bob-white!*

From the top of the trail came the answer, *Bob, bob-white.* Out of the forest came Knut, Brian, Mart, and Jim.

"What did you do, fly up here?" Jim panted.

"Deer trail," Hallie answered briefly. "We have everything under control."

"We caught both Fred and Opie," Trixie added.

"Have they told you where Tank and Cap are?" Knut asked.

By this time, Ron had joined the exhausted Bob-Whites. "Trixie figured that out on the way up. Come on to the mine, fellows, and we'll set them free."

In a straggling row, they passed a neatly fenced-in stake with Tank's name on it, *Anders Anderson.* Trixie did not know what she expected a gold mine to look like, but certainly nothing so ordinary as a slag heap, some old wheelbarrows, picks and shovels, and a handmade door set into the side of a very deep gully.

Hallie and Knut were first to reach the door.

"It's locked!" Hallie yelled.

"What did you expect, a welcome mat?" asked Knut.

"How can we get in?" Di wailed.

"I thought this might happen," said Ron, "so I brought along Tank's ax." After much hacking, he was able to remove the hinges from the door frame. Mart and Brian opened the door from the hinge side and dragged it across dirt.

"Tank!" Knut bellowed. "Are you in there?"

For a long second, there was only silence.

"Cap? Tank? Where are you?" Hallie screamed.

"Back here, dad blame it!" came the feeble but testy answer. Sobbing hoarsely, Hallie snatched Mart's flashlight and rushed into the cold, damp dark.

The others followed more carefully. They found Tank sprawled on a folded tarp, with one ankle chained to the wall. Beside him was a pail of water, a burned-out lantern, and a skunk that thumped an angry warning on the rock floor.

"Is that Mister or Loverly?" Knut asked as he edged forward cautiously.

The old miner shielded his eyes from the light and managed a weak chuckle. "It's me Loverly."

Hallie knelt to hug Tank's thin shoulders. "Tank, oh, Tank," she crooned. "Are you all right? Where's Cap?" While she patted and murmured, the others managed to set Tank free from his chain.

"Does it hurt, sir?" asked Brian. "Will you be able to stand?"

Tank held up wrinkled hands knotted with arthritis. "Let me see vhat ay can do."

Willing hands helped Tank to his feet. He wobbled toward the oblong of early morning light at the end of the tunnel, leaning heavily on Mart and Knut.

Hallie carried Loverly and kept saying, "Where's Cap? Where's Cap? Isn't anybody going to set Cap free?"

Once outdoors, Tank shook free of supporting hands. Shivering, he wrapped long arms around his rib cage. "Ain't been so cold since ay locked meself inside me own ice cave," Tank admitted. He accepted the sweater Jim took off. "Now, vhat's this yammerin' about Cap? Vhy'd ya tank he vas vith me?"

"Y-You mean, he isn't?" Hallie stammered.

Safe at Last! • 20

EVERYONE RUSHED back to the cabin to shout questions at the tied-up Swishers. The father and son simply stared back and kept their mouths shut. "We're not tellin' a thing," Opie said sullenly. "All our plans are shot to ribbons, so why should you get anything? I was all set to kill me a bigfoot and get my name in the history books, and Fred here was going to find him some gold. We'd be rich and famous—whooey! It isn't fair that nothing's panned out for us."

"Let's search the grounds," Trixie urged. "They may have Cap chained someplace, too."

It didn't take long to search the claim, the

pump house, ice cave, and woodshed. There was no sign of Cap.

"We have to go back to camp and start our search from there," Trixie decided. "But what about the Swishers?"

"Yust leave them to me!" Tank said grimly. The old miner stood in his own doorway and glared at the uninvited guests on the floor.

"I just remembered," said Ron. "Sheriff Sprute promised me he'd be in camp by daylight. He should be coming any minute. I'll stick around here until he arrives to pick up our prisoners."

Di had gone straight to Tank's stove, where Mart was helping her build a fire. "No one's going anywhere till we eat," she said. "If it's all right with you, Tank, I'll cook whatever you suggest."

"Little lady," Tank said gently, "you're velcome to anyt'ing ay own."

With many hands to do the work, everyone was soon breakfasting on huge slices of ham, hot biscuits with wild honey, and mugs of hot chocolate. Brian insisted that Tank drink soup, with only a few bites of solid food.

Trixie finished eating and turned to Tank. "I've been wondering about your fur suit that Fred stole. If you don't mind my asking—"

Tank's chuckle interrupted her. "Me bones always freeze up in the marrow, come vinter," he explained. "This time ay fix that. Ay stretched me some pelts and ay cut me some varm, fur yammers—"

"Yammers?" Di repeated.

"Pajamas," Hallie whispered.

"But they disappeared 'fore ay got 'em zippered up. Then ay had me a fight on my hands. Ay lost." He glanced at the tumbled mess of all his belongings and the hole in his cabin floor. He grinned slyly. "But ay tank they didn't find me gold, yah?"

"Yah," Knut and Hallie answered, being glad with him.

Trixie squirmed.

"Ay tank the young lady vould like to know me hiding place," guessed Tank.

Trixie nodded eagerly.

Tank scowled at the Swishers. "Everyone but them, come on outside."

The young people trooped out the door, burning with curiosity to know where Tank would hide the savings of a lifetime.

Tank leaned his bald head close and whispered, "It's hidden in chunks of ice in the bottom of me ice cave!"

Trixie giggled with delight. "That's perfect!

Gleeps, I'm so glad we closed the cave door after Fred had left it open!"

"Me, too," Tank said quietly. "And ay tank tomorrow ay'll be carting that gold to the bank."

"Oh, Tank, that's wonderful," said Hallie, giving him another squeeze.

"Yah, vell, ay tank de tistles be tick dis year, yah?"

"Yah, sure," echoed the Bob-Whites softly.

Knut pointed out a helicopter whacking air as close to a mountain as it dared to fly. "Sheriff Sprute's on the job," Knut said briefly.

"About time." Hallie's voice dripped acid.

"Cap disappeared late Wednesday afternoon, and this is only Friday morning," said Knut, trying to be reasonable.

"Only!" Di's voice cracked from weariness. "It feels like forever."

Her exhausted companions agreed, but stoically waved good-bye to Tank and Ron and headed down the mountain.

It seemed to Trixie that the usual two hours downhill to camp were endless. Long before they reached Champion Creek, Trixie could smell smoke and knew that either Miss Trask had survived her night alone in camp, or else the forest was on fire. The group stumbled into camp to find that Miss Trask had heard them coming and had sausages cooking and eggs ready to scramble.

"The sheriff has been here," she told them as she doled out orange juice. "He is out now, assigning sections to his searchers, but he'll be back."

"We found Tank," Trixie said, "and tied up the Swishers. But—"

"But we didn't find Cap," Hallie finished bleakly. "Where can that birdbrain be?"

Miss Trask swallowed carefully, her face twisted with aching sympathy. Then she smiled and pointed a shaking finger toward the road. Amazed by Miss Trask's strange reaction to Hallie's words, the others turned their heads to stare past the tents.

Cap Belden was entering the campground!

"Capelton?" Knut faltered.

"*Cap!*" Hallie screamed.

The Bob-Whites watched the three Beldens tighten arms around waists, heads close together. Then they, too, ran to meet Cap. "We thought the sasquatch got you!" Di cried.

"That fraud?" Cap scoffed.

"Where have you been?" Hallie demanded. "We've worn grooves on that mountain, hunting for you."

"I've been walking from Cedar Mountain," Cap said.

"Cedar?" Hallie fluttered a hand that pointed west.

"That's a heck of a hike from here!" Knut whistled.

"You're telling me," Cap said wearily. "Can't I sit down before I fall down?" Stiffly he plodded and dropped into the first chair he reached. He stretched out both legs, leaned back, and closed his eyes. Brown hairs fuzzed his jaws and upper lip. He had lost the thong that usually tied his long brown hair. Scratched, bruised, and dirty, Cap Belden was the most beautiful sight Trixie had ever seen.

Trixie saw that Cap's feet were bound with pieces of leather, tied with knotted thongs that had to be the long fringes from his handsome jacket. "Why did you whack up your jacket?" she asked. "Where are your shoes?"

Cap looked regretful. "After I got away from one Swisher, another one clobbered me with the butt of his shotgun. They loaded me in that old wagon they racket around in and took me to that deserted logging camp on Cedar Mountain. They stole my moccasins and dumped me. I worked my way out of their ropes. I've been walking ever since, but it was good-bye jacket, hello foot bindings—or I wouldn't have made it. I could use some food, though."

Hallie bustled about, eyes glowing with black fire. Her mouth could not stop smiling. She declared proudly, "I told everyone that Cap could live off the land!"

"Just barely," Cap mumbled.

After Cap had eaten, the exhausted campers sank into bedrolls for the first truly untroubled sleep since their adventures had begun.

Trixie slept peacefully, comforted to know that Cap was safe, and so was old Tank. Once, midway between dream and waking, she marveled at the oneness with environment possessed by those two—a sixteen-year-old mountain man and an eighty-year-old hard-rock miner. If their environment included a real sasquatch from this time forward, she knew they would live with it and not against it.

"And I hope there is," Trixie mumbled.

"Is what, Trix?"

Trixie's round blue eyes flew open, but she saw no monster's face. Honey was bending over her bed, telling her that it was nearly time for the Bob-Whites to join Knut and Gloria on their date.

"A sasquatch," Trixie answered. "I hope it's really real."

Hope? Why had she used that word? She *had* seen the strange beast of the forest at first light of dawn and at noon. She had heard its cries and had known its scent. Soon her name would be added to the long, long list of people whose lives had been changed by a sight, a sound, or an odor. Until the mystery was solved in a laboratory, Trixie could cling to the memory of something incredibly ancient, dimly seen, and beyond understanding.